Penguin Books

State of the Heart

Rhonda is the answer to all Robert's problems, or so he thinks; Andy's certain his fantasies are about to come true when he's asked to fix a tap; Emma's legs need shaving but her mother won't let her do it; and Jonathan can't help wondering how couples in films get out of their clothes so quickly and easily!

These wonderfully entertaining stories tell of the confusion, ecstasy, pain and anxiety of growing up and falling in love. With great humour, wit and insight, established authors reveal the state of the adolescent heart in a way that everyone will recognize and hugely enjoy.

State of the Heart

Compiled by
P. E. MATTHEWS

PENGUIN BOOKS

PENGUIN BOOKS

Published by the Penguin Group
Penguin Books Ltd, 27 Wrights Lane, London W8 5TZ, England
Penguin Books USA Inc., 375 Hudson Street, New York, New York 10014, USA
Penguin Books Australia Ltd, Ringwood, Victoria, Australia
Penguin Books Canada Ltd, 10 Alcorn Avenue, Toronto, Ontario, Canada M4V 3B2
Penguin Books (NZ) Ltd, 182–190 Wairau Road, Auckland 10, New Zealand

Penguin Books Ltd, Registered Offices: Harmondsworth, Middlesex, England

First published by Omnibus Books, Adelaide,
in association with Penguin Books Australia Limited 1988
First published in Great Britain by Viking Books 1990
Published in Penguin Books 1992
1 3 5 7 9 10 8 6 4 2

This collection copyright © Omnibus Books, 1988
Copyright in individual stories is retained by the authors
All rights reserved

Printed in England by Clays Ltd, St Ives plc

Except in the United States of America, this book is sold subject
to the condition that it shall not, by way of trade or otherwise, be lent,
re-sold, hired out, or otherwise circulated without the publisher's
prior consent in any form of binding or cover other than that in
which it is published and without a similar condition including this
condition being imposed on the subsequent purchaser

Contents

Love Among the Moccasins
Max Dann   1

The Plumber
Allan Baillie   13

Love Letters
Kate Walker   23

I Remember Gloria
Norman Marks   31

First Love
Geoff Goodfellow   41

The Flea
Peter McFarlane   51

The Black-and-White Boy
Gillian Rubinstein   65

How Do They Get Cranes on Top of Tall Buildings?
Doug MacLeod   79

First Impressions
Nette Hilton   93

Sandra
Max Dann — 105

D.G. Loves A.R. True!
Dianne Bates — 115

Down the Mall
Sally Farrell Odgers — 125

Jonathon's Story
Nette Hilton — 137

Love Among the Moccasins

Max Dann

I was seventeen, girl crazy, and depressed.

I was girl crazy because I was seventeen, depressed because I was girl crazy, and seventeen because I happened to have been sixteen the year before. I had no choice in that.

I was prepared to go to any length to get myself a girlfriend. Nothing was too much trouble. Get engaged, marry, turn Catholic, travel interstate, wear away my face washing it with Phisohex four times a day—anything at all.

I could fall in love with anyone. She didn't even have to look particularly like a girl—as long as she had a girl's name was enough.

I was handing out friendship rings like they were lollies. I was giving my number to complete strangers, then watching the phone for days at a time. I knew so many girls who just wanted to be friends I could have stood for a seat in parliament.

My father used to call me Tyrone Powerless. He was very sympathetic.

It hardly seemed worth going on.

Until I met Rhonda. I fell in love the moment I saw her. She was immaculate. She was tall, and cool, and poised, and mysterious, and intelligent, and witty, and graceful, and attractive.

She had this wispy baby-fine hair in long drop curls. And a pale, pale complexion. So smooth and unmarked it looked as though it had never been taken out anywhere before.

The only trouble was, I couldn't talk to her. I suffered total loss of speech within a ten-metre radius.

We worked at the same factory, in the same room, at opposite benches. We even did the same job: sticking sheepskin insoles to partly assembled moccasin leathers. We'd do a pair at a time, stuff them into a plastic bag, toss in a small ball of white string, some brief instructions and a needle, and staple it up. People would buy them and then spend the next three winters bent over in their lounge-rooms trying to figure out how they went together.

Occasionally I'd see Rhonda outside from across the street, getting her lunch or something. She'd wave. A big, friendly, "How are you? Gee, it's great to see you, Howdy doody" sort of wave. Ten minutes later we'd be standing practically on top of each other and she wouldn't utter a word. It was very confusing.

I was becoming desperate. All I'd managed in three months was 500 "Good morning"s, and a flamboyant wave once or twice a week.

But I did have one thing going for me. Douglas Grose. He worked out in despatch. He knew everything there was to know about women. He had five sisters at home.

"You're wasting your time," he said when I told him about Rhonda. "She's out of your league. Way out of your class."

Douglas Grose had this real knack of boosting up your confidence when you most needed it.

We were sitting in the lunch room, just the two of us. It was a room full of atmosphere. Four Laminex tables, chairs to go with them, a sink, an urn, six cupboards, ashtrays, and a window.

I went on telling Douglas about my problems while he ate his lunch. He had the worst looking lunches I've ever seen in my life. He had a main course that lasted thirty seconds, and that took up about an eighth of his bag. The rest was all dessert. Three or four chocolate bars, a couple of cream cakes, a packet of licorice allsorts, an eskimo pie, a bag of chocolate-covered sultanas, and a bottle of caramel-flavoured milk. Often he'd have two or three different things going at once. It was awful to watch.

"Now let me see if I've got this straight," he was saying. "You haven't taken her out, you haven't told her how you feel, and you haven't talked to her yet?" He took a bite of his cream finger and added, "What have you been doing all this time, using telepathic communication?"

"I can't decide where to take her," I said.

"Take her to the pictures."

"I can't just ask her along to some stupid movie. It'd have to be somewhere special with her. I was thinking more of dinner."

"Forget it. You have to do too much talking at dinner. You're not the talkative type. The pictures is where you should go. All you have to worry about then is travel time there, a bit more conversation at interval, and making it back home again."

"What could I take her to see?"

"Something you hate. Find the last movie you'd ever think of going to, and take her to that. Girls have got no taste when it comes to pictures."

He thought for a moment while he started clearing up his wrappers and bags.

"Once you get talking, the rest will come natural. Then just sort of bring movies into the conversation, gradually. Something like, 'Say, there's a great new film in town. Have you heard about it? Maybe we should go together.'"

He made it sound so easy I decided I'd do it. I'd ask her out that very afternoon.

There was a quiet time around three o'clock. Half the stickers in the room were at their afternoon tea break. An audience of three had to be better than one of eight.

I waited for the right moment.

Now? No, not yet. Wait until she was finished stapling. Now? Hang on, hang on, all right. Ten seconds. Start the count down: 9, 8, 7, 6, 5, 4, 3, 2, 1.

"When do you think they'll get the new lino in the lunch room?"

She didn't look up straight away. It took her a while to realise it was me talking to her. Then she stared at me. Straight at me. She wasn't going to say anything back. I was beginning to feel warm all over. I looked down. I'd been brushing the same insole for fifteen minutes. I'd put enough glue on it to stick down every moccasin leather in Melbourne.

"I didn't know they were putting any in."

She'd spoken! She'd said something to me! It was my turn again.

"Yes, they've been talking about it for some time now." I was feeling about as casual as a three-piece suit.

"Oh."

"I think it's been needed for quite a while myself."

"I've never noticed one way or another."

"No, neither have I really. I mean, I wouldn't have at all if it hadn't been pointed out to me in the first place. Of course I've glanced at it every now and then, but hardly ever."

What was I doing talking about lino? Some conversation.

I looked at my watch. Four minutes before the room filled up again. How was I going to get from lino to movies in four minutes? I'd have to improvise.

"Have you ever seen *Ben Hur*?"

"No."

"Oh. How about *Little Big Man*?"

"I hate westerns."

"So do I, so do I. I hate westerns too. How about *Summer of '42*, seen that?"

She shook her head.

"Neither have I."

Here it was. The line I'd been waiting to use. It was shuffling its way from the back stalls to the front. It was taking its time, too.

"Maybe we could go and see it together?"

I'd done it! I'd said it! I could have stapled up my thumb inside one of the bags and not noticed it was missing. I was so excited I could barely go on standing there. Something electric, ticklish, was rushing up and down me. It felt like I had on mohair underwear. I was Steve McQueen, Dustin Hoffman and Robert Redford all rolled into one.

The only thing was, she hadn't answered. Hadn't said a thing.

I could hear the second shift dragging their feet down the hall. Rhonda was back sticking her next pair. She wasn't looking up any more. Maybe she hadn't heard me? I couldn't stand that. I couldn't go through all that again.

The other stickers arrived back and took their positions around the benches again. Well, that was that. It was over. Hopeless. Trying to have a conversation with them standing there was about as private as going on national television.

"OK."

I looked up.

"OK, I'll come. How's Saturday?"

Now she was asking me.

"Saturday? Saturday would be just perfect. Just great. Yep, Saturday is OK with me. Saturday is my favourite day to go out."

"Will you pick me up?"

I could feel the eyes and hear the slowed, hushed brush strokes of everybody in the room. It was so quiet I could even hear the cardboard boxes being folded out in despatch. There wouldn't be a person in the place who didn't know every word of this by the morning.

"Sure. Where do you live?"

"One twenty-three Frawley Street, Frankston. Is that too far?"

"Oh no, Frankston isn't too far. Frankston is no trouble. I know Frankston inside out."

Frankston! Where was Frankston? I knew it was down near a beach or something. It didn't sound like it was anywhere near Footscray though.

I was at her place at 6.32. She'd said 6.30, but Douglas Grose had told me to be a little late. I'd been browsing through the magazines down at the milk bar on the corner for twenty-five minutes to make sure.

She met me at the door. She looked great. She had on a red-and-white striped dress and bright red lipstick.

She hesitated at the front gate, like she was looking around for something.

"Where did you park your car?"

"I haven't got a car," I said.

"Oh, you've got a motor bike!"

"Train."

"You're taking me out by train?"

She didn't seem all that pleased. I don't know why she was acting so bothered. I'd been catching buses and trams and trains since two o'clock in the afternoon trying to get there from Footscray on time. I must have passed through every suburb in Melbourne.

It took so long to get into the city that we only just managed to get tickets.

I'd never sat in the very front row before.

The first half of the programme was mostly taken up by a documentary about an English battleship on trials and how much fun the crew had with the guns and everything.

Very romantic.

We went out to the foyer at interval, and I couldn't think of a thing to say. Nothing. Usually I could come up with something. But the harder I tried, the less that came.

I almost thought of one thing. But it had to do with the carpet. I didn't want to get on to discussing floor coverings again. So I went and got us ice creams.

Everybody wanted an ice cream. I almost killed myself

getting them. Getting served at one of those counters is like doing a crash course in assertiveness. If you don't yell and push, you could wind up standing there right through the main feature. Which wouldn't have been such a bad thing that night.

Let me tell you something about *Summer of '42*, if you haven't seen it. Sentimental? It was the unhappiest hour and forty-two minutes of my life. Getting run over would have been funnier. Everybody was crying. I was surrounded by people sniffing and blowing away into hankies. I missed whole bits of it because of the noise. I probably would have cried myself if I hadn't been thinking about something else.

I'd waited until it was about half way through to make my move. Then, very casually, I lifted my right arm, lowered it into position, and slid it across the back of her seat.

It was a long way off to her shoulder. It felt like I was mailing my hand to Sydney. I felt the edge of the seat where it curved over, and rested it there. It had taken ten minutes to do that much.

After a while I let my hand slip on to her shoulder. No response. She didn't move, or flinch, or lean my way, nothing! I might as well have been trying to make friends with a weatherboard fence.

For nearly an hour my arm just hung there. Lost in the darkness over by her far shoulder somewhere. I should have brought it back. But you know how it is at the pictures. Every time you make a little move it feels like you're tossing around somebody's good plates. Besides, I was sure everybody for three rows back had seen me manoeuvre it there. I didn't want to make a spectacle of myself pulling it away again.

We didn't have time for coffee or anything. We had to catch the first train back we could.

"She was great, wasn't she?"

"Who?"

"Jennifer O'Neil," I said. "The star."

"I didn't like her."

The train finally pulled out of the station. I thought I'd try again.

"You can certainly see a lot when you're sitting up close, though, can't you?"

"All I could see was a couple of blurry shapes moving back and forth."

She was exaggerating a little.

"And my neck is killing me. I thought it was never going to end."

She'd have been wonderful to take away on a trip somewhere.

We could have gone on chatting like that for hours. Only the carriage filled up when we stopped at Richmond.

I'd never seen so many hoodlums and sharpies and vandals and street bashers and murderers all such good friends before. Eight hundred of them. We were just lucky that they picked our carriage to sit in, I suppose. They were on their way back to Frankston too.

Rhonda knew one or two of them. She knew one particularly well. His name was Razor Blade.

He came over to where we were sitting. I thought he'd been stabbed in the stomach at first. But it was just the way he sneered all the time.

He was leaning over from the seat in front, giving us a demonstration of his bad breath.

"I haven't seen you around for a while, Rhonda."

He could talk through his nose without moving his mouth.

"You just haven't known where to look."

"I've been missing you," he said.

"It's a bit late for that now, isn't it?"

Why was I beginning to feel so uncomfortable?

"Don't ever say it's too late. It's never too late," he snapped.

"It's been six months since you rang last. Am I supposed to

stay home and wait?"

"Maybe I'll give you a ring tomorrow," he said.

He had a wonderful set of teeth. He must have had at least seven or eight there.

"Ring all you like. Don't count on me answering though."

Razor turned around to see what his friends were doing. They seemed to be enjoying themselves. Ripping open seats, breaking windows, carving their names in the woodwork. He turned back.

"Who's the jerk?"

I was pretty sure it was me. I could tell by the finger poking into my chest and the close-up view I had of his chin.

"He's nobody," Rhonda said. "He's just a young friend from work. He wanted to see a movie and I took him, that's all."

Oh great, great. That made me feel fantastic.

"What's his name?"

"Robert."

He swung back across to me. "What did you want to go and see, Robby?"

Why did she have to say *I* wanted to go and see it?

"*Summer of '42*," I mumbled.

He laughed. His mouth even stayed the same for that. He'd really perfected that sneer.

"Hey, Monkey, come over here," he called out.

Monkey was short and had long arms. They were the longest arms I'd ever seen. It would have been impossible for him to trip over.

"Now tell him what you just went to see!"

"*Summer of '42*," I mumbled again.

Monkey didn't seem to know how to laugh. He tried, but his mouth got caught on something and he ended up looking like a barracuda.

"Tell me, Robby," Razor went on, "did you see *My Fair Lady* too?"

"I missed that."

He grabbed my shirt at the neck and leaned over even more, until we were almost kissing. He only got worse closer up.

"You're not being smart, are you?"

Some people are impossible to please. Even when you tell them the truth they don't believe you.

"Leave him alone. He's just a kid," Rhonda said. She folded her arms and looked out the window. "If you think you're impressing me by hurting him, you're not."

"I'm not hurting him. Am I hurting you, Robby?"

Actually my throat was getting a little sore. I'm just thankful I didn't have my top button done up.

He let go after a while. I suppose his hand must have got tired.

I could go on and tell you about the rest of the trip. How Razor went on talking to Rhonda and I couldn't get a word in. And then give a couple of vivid descriptions of Monkey practising his Chinese burns on me, and what a great bunch they all were. But I'd rather not.

Or I could tell you what happened when I finally got Rhonda home. How she wouldn't talk to me and I missed the last train home and had to walk. And was still walking at ten o'clock Sunday morning because I took a wrong turn at Moorabbin and was almost in Balwyn before I realised.

But there's no sense in going into any of that either.

I'll just go straight to the epilogue.

Well, it all turned out OK. Rhonda and I finished up by living happily ever after. Everything worked out fine. She got married to a plumber and moved up to the Gold Coast. And me? I got married to Anne. She was one of the stickers on the bench just over from Rhonda and me. Or didn't I mention her?

The Plumber

Allan Baillie

He must be a butcher, Andy thought. A mad Neanderthal with hair all over him. Possessive as hell. Probably carries that scabbard full of knives everywhere he goes, clinking with every step. Probably keeps it under the bed. With the cleaver.

Andy shivered.

He was sprawled high on a lonely curve of North Avalon Beach, so early in the morning the sun was still touching the sea. He was watching a lithe brown woman in a gold bikini—maybe twenty-five years old, no more—jogging alone on the wet sand. He was thinking of her husband.

She must have a husband, he thought. Probably got five kids at home. Bawling. No, no kids at all. That's why she can be here now, instead of running round the kitchen.

Tossing her long brown hair—was it auburn?—back over her shoulder. Kicking a light spray of sand back, and the little bounce with every step. That was lovely.

Andy sat up.

Probably a teacher.

He sagged on to his knees.

One of the new ones you're going to have to put up with this year. Oh yeah, that would be great, wouldn't it?

The woman was turning now, before the life-saving club, and coming back.

Well, why not? What are you gunna do?

Andy stood up as the woman approached, and brushed the sand from his togs. He felt strangely wobbly.

He's probably in the dunes with binoculars and the cleaver. The husband.

Andy began to jog to the surf, thrusting out his chest, working his biceps slightly. The woman noticed him and faltered in her run, a ghost of unease drifting across her face.

"Great day, ennit?" he said, as he passed her and hit the surf. He looked back, and she was smiling at him until he dived.

See, that wasn't all that bad, was it? That was a warm, friendly smile. Glad we did it.

He surfaced with a raised arm to wave at the woman, to say something else, but she had gone on jogging.

Still, that was a beginning.

The next day he walked to the surf, waved, and said: "Another great day."

And she said: "Lovely."

The next day he was swimming when she came to the beach and was drying himself as she came past the second time. He said: "Hi again."

And she said: "You look cold."

And he said quickly, before she had gone past: "There's a cold current out there." He had been in the water, waiting for the woman, for half an hour. "But it's all right when you get used to it. Don't you ever go in?"

She shook her head and called back: "I'm frightened of the surf."

The next day he was squatting at the tide-line, watching the sun on the horizon. He said: "You don't want to be frightened of the sea."

And she stopped. "I'm not. I'm frightened of the surf."

"Oh." Andy searched for something else to say.

"You on holidays?"

Her eyes—brown eyes—were wandering all over his face, a spray of freckles crossed her snub nose, her mouth looked like it was about to break into laughter . . .

"Oh, yes, sort of."

"From school?"

"Sort of."

She nodded and prepared to run off.

"I'm Andy."

"Oh, yes . . ."

"Well, you know, since we keep on running into each other . . ."

"I'm Else."

"Something Else?"

And Else laughed. The freckles danced across her nose, her eyes sparkled, those lips quivered and parted. "Else Something," she said and jogged away.

But next day rain swept in from the sea and Andy swam alone. For three days after that the sea was hammered into glowering submission by downpours from a swollen purple sky. Finally the sun returned. Without Else.

After three more days Andy stopped kicking about the beach, stopped picturing laughing Else in the paws of her ape of a husband, and went back to school. He was walking home from a mate's home when he found her.

She was weeding the garden in front of a white stucco house, squatting in short shorts. Andy stopped on the footpath and felt his heart lurch.

Melons, so small, the cotton'll never hold—stop that! What d'you say, come on, come on . . .

Else looked up and around. "Oh, hi." She frowned. "Hi, Harry."

"Andy. Missed you, Else."

"Bit of trouble. Nice to see you." She was looking him over, as if she had never seen him before.

"Oh. Sorry about that. About the trouble. Didn't know you lived so close to the beach."

"That was all the bastard left me." With a quick smile.

The bastard? The Neanderthal, he exists after all. But there was something in Else's eyes now.

"You going to get down to the beach again, Else?"

"I don't know, Andy. S'pose I should." She steadied herself on a trowel.

Andy dropped his eyes to the opening of Else's shirt and forced them away. "It's good this week. The tide's—"

"What're you like on plumbing, Andy?" Else spoke low and fast. As if she had just made her mind up about something and didn't want anyone to know.

"Plumbing?"

"I've got this terrible dripping tap in the kitchen. Do you know about these things?"

Something's happening! Electricity in the air. Jesus . . .

"Oh sure." Keep it calm, terribly calm.

"Would you have time to look at it, Andy?"

You, for sure, are kidding! "Yeah, sure."

Else almost leaped to her feet, put her soil-encrusted fingers on Andy's shoulders, and hustled him off the footpath and round the back. As if she was kidnapping him. Andy felt the warmth of her fingers through his shirt, smelt the tang of her sweat, and did not mind being kidnapped at all.

She took hold of his hand beside the garage, pulled him across the quarry-tiled patio and into a dazzling white kitchen. She let him go and stood facing him, and said: "What do you think?"

What, do you grab her and kiss her? Now?

Standing terribly close with those still, watching eyes and the mouth just lifted at the corner.

But you don't know her. She might shout and slap your face and kick you out the house. And tell her Neanderthal and— even worse—the parents!

"This the tap?"

A sound like a sigh. "Yes."

"Doesn't look like it drips much."

Else reached out and cuffed the tap and a few drips splattered the sink. "It comes and goes. Would you like a drink?"

"A drink? Oh, sure." You got to get it right.

Else stepped away from Andy and opened the fridge door. She took out two cans of beer and passed one to Andy.

"Thanks."

"I don't usually drink beer, but since he left it here I might as well, hey?"

"Yeah."

That's right. He left. The Neanderthal isn't here any more. So what do you do?

Else pulled the ring tab, gulped the beer and smiled at him over the top of the can. He joined her clumsily.

"Well, what do you want to do, Andy?" Hiding her mouth behind the can, a pixie.

You're frightened, aren't you, kid? Really frightened.

"Nice beer, thanks. Your—he left it here?"

The light left Else's face. "Gone. Vanished. With his scented lady. Don't worry about him. Now . . .?"

Else looked at Andy, steadily, motionless.

Andy stared at her, at the slowly moving breasts, the glistening lips trailing a trace of beer foam, the waiting eyes.

And he said: "Have you a spare washer?"

She blinked. "A washer?"

"To fix the tap. It's easy. I've helped Dad lots of times. Just unscrew the tap, take out the old washer, put in the new one, and that's it."

"Are you sure you want to do this?"

"Only take a moment. Really. Got a washer?"

Just need a minute. To get it all worked out.

"Probably." She pulled out a drawer quickly and showed him a mound on a metal stem, a small mushroom. "That it?"

"That's it. And tools?"

Else walked out of the kitchen.

Andy held up his hands and watched them shake.

Oh boy, you got it made, wait until you tell the guys. No, you don't do that. Just nod and smile when they get to talking. Just stop shivering.

He swept his hands to the round piece of shining metal at the base of the tap and began to turn it. Else returned with a dusty toolbox.

"That enough?"

"Oh, fine. Thanks." He rummaged in the box and came up with a wrench. He locked it on the large nut behind the metal disc and heaved at it. Else stood at his elbow.

It's moving. It's going to be finished in a couple of minutes, and what are you going to do then, eh? What you're going to do is put the wrench on the sink and turn round and say: "Well, Else, that's finished, no trouble. Now is there anything else I can do?" And she is going to be standing so close she will be breathing into you. "Thanks, Andy," she will say. "Well, there is—" And you won't let her say another word, right? You will put your arms around her and draw her body into yours and kiss her for a long, long time. Feel her soft warmth against you, her fingers at your back. She will then push you gently away, smile and lead you to her bed . . .

Andy brought the wrench down and happily watched a spray grow around the nut. Then the spray exploded into a fierce jet, hurling the nut against his chest. Else squealed and thrust her hand across the jet to where the tap had been.

"What's happened?" she screamed.

"Forgot to turn the water off!" shouted Andy in anguish. "I'll fix it!" He ran through the house to the front door.

He found the main water tap at the edge of the garden and turned it off in less than a minute and replaced the old washer with the new in no more than five. Too late. When he turned from the tap she was looking at the pool at her feet, the spray across the cupboards and ceiling, the muddy footprints on the white carpet in the corridor and the greasy fingerprints on a corner.

"It's finished," he said. "Sorry."

"That's all right, Andy. No damage. Thank you for the tap." She shook his hand. "Would you turn the water on as you go?"

Andy walked round the house, turned the main tap on, plodded down the street and stopped before a high brick wall.

And he began to methodically bang his head.

Love Letters

Kate Walker

My name's Nick and my chick's name's Fleur. And she has a friend called Helen who's got a boyfriend named Clive. Now this Clive is really weird. Well, he does one weird thing I know of anyway: he writes three-page letters to his girlfriend, Helen, *every* day.

"What's wrong with the nerd?" I asked Fleur. She'd spent a whole lunch time telling me about him.

"There's nothing *wrong* with him," she said. "You're so unromantic, Nick."

"Of course I'm not unromantic!" I said, and I offered her a lick of my ice cream to prove it. She groaned and pulled her PE bag over her head. She didn't want to talk to me any more.

When girls go quiet, that's a bad sign!

"What's wrong?" I asked her.

"You don't love me," she said.

"Of course I love you," I told her. I offered her my whole ice cream. She wouldn't take it.

"You don't love me *enough*," she said.

"How much is *enough*?"

How much ice cream did it take?

"You don't write *me* letters like Clive does to Helen," she said.

"I don't need to, I see you every day in Computers," I said. "*And* Chemistry."

"Clive sees Helen every day in Biology, and Textiles, and Home Science, and assembly, and roll call," she said, "and he writes letters to *her* !"

I knew what was happening here: my girlfriend was cooling on me.

"OK," I said, "I'll write you a letter."
"Aw, Nick!" She whipped her PE bag off her head.

I was glad I'd weakened. Fleur is really gorgeous. I couldn't risk losing her for the sake of a few lines scrawled on a piece of paper. I'm the envy of the boys' locker room, having her for a girlfriend.

I sat down that night and began my first letter: "Dear Fleur . . ." Then I stared at the page for the next half hour. What do you write in letters to someone you see every day? I chewed my pencil; I chewed my nails. Then, in desperation, I finally asked Mum.

"Write about the things you have in common," Mum said, so I wrote the following: "Wasn't that computer class on Tuesday a ROAR? The best bit was when Brando tilted the computer to show us the little button underneath and the monitor fell off."

I wrote about the Chemistry class too, though it wasn't quite as interesting. Not a single kid muffed their experiment and blew their eyebrows off. But then I got really creative at the end of the letter and added a postscript written in Basic.

I got the letter back next day with "five-and-a-half out of twenty" marked on the bottom.

"What was wrong with it?" I asked Fleur.

"You made a lot of spelling mistakes for one thing," she said.

"I was being *myself*!" I told her.

"I didn't notice," she said. "You didn't say anything *personal* in it!"

Is that what she wanted, a *personal* letter?

I thought it over for five minutes. There were guys all round the lunch area just waiting to take my place and share their chocolate milk with the fabulous Fleur. If revealing a few personal secrets was what it took to keep her, I could do it.

"Dear Fleur . . ." I began the second letter that night, "This is not something I'd tell everyone, but I use a deodorant. Only on sports days or in really hot weather of course."

No, that was too personal. I ripped up the page and started again. "Dear Fleur, Guess what? Mrs Hessel blew me up in History today for no reason at all. I was embarrassed to death. Goggle-eyes Gilda laughed her stupid head off."

Actually, once I'd got started I found the personal stuff not that hard to write. I told Fleur what mark I'd *really* got in the English half-yearlies. Then I told her about a movie I'd seen where this pioneer farming guy loses his plough horse, then loses his wife, then his children, and then his cows get hoof rot. But even though he sits down and bawls his eyes out about it, in the end he walks off into the sunset, a stronger man.

"I'd like to suffer a great personal loss like that," I told Fleur in the letter, "and walk away stronger and nobler for it."

Her sole comment on letter number two was: "You didn't say anything in it about *me*." And she went off to eat lunch with Helen.

It was time to hit the panic button. Fleur was "drifting". I stuffed my sandwiches back in my bag and went looking for Clive. I bailed him up under the stairwell.

"OK, what do you put in your letters to Helen?" I asked him.

Clive turned out to be a decent kid. He not only told me, he gave me a photocopy of the latest letter he was writing to Helen.

You should have seen it!

"Darling Helen, Your hair is like gold. Your eyes remind me of twilight reflected on Throsby Creek. Your ear lobes are . . . Your eyelashes are . . ." And so on. It was what you'd call a poetic autopsy.

And as if that wasn't bad enough, he then got into the

declarations of love: "You're special to me because . . . I yearn for you in History because . . . I can't eat noodles without thinking of you because . . ."

"Do girls really go for this sort of thing?" I asked him.

"Helen does," he said. "She'd drop me tomorrow if I stopped writing her letters. It's the price you pay if you want to keep your girlfriend."

So I began my third letter, with Clive's photocopy propped up in front of me as a guide.

"Dear Fleur, Your hair is like . . ." I began.

Actually, I'd always thought it was like fairy-floss, pretty from a distance but all gooey when you touched it—too much hair-spray, I suppose.

I scrapped that opening and started again.

"Dear Fleur, Your eyes are like . . ."

Actually, they're a bit small and squinty. I think she might need glasses but she's not letting on.

Scrub the eyes.

"Dear Fleur, Your face is excellent overall. You look like one of those soap-opera dolls."

I thought I would've been able to go on for hours about her face, but having said that, it seemed to sum her up.

I moved on to the declarations: "I love you because . . ." I chewed my pencil again, then my fingernails. This time I couldn't ask Mum.

Why did I love Fleur? Because she was spunky. Because all the guys thought so too. Well, not all of them. Some of them thought she wasn't all that interesting to talk to, but I put that down to jealousy.

Still, I began to wonder, what *had* we talked about in the three weeks we'd been going together? Not much really. She'd never been interested enough in my hockey playing to ask in-depth questions about it. And, I have to admit, I hadn't found her conversation on white ankle boots all that riveting either.

No wonder I was having so much trouble writing letters to her. We had nothing in common. I barely knew her. What were her views on nuclear disarmament? Maybe she didn't have any. Was she pro-Libyan? I didn't know.

I scrapped the letter, scrapped Clive's photocopy, and started again, this time with no trouble at all.

"Dear Fleur, This writing of letters was a very good idea because it gives me the opportunity to say something important to you. I think you're a nice girl and I've enjoyed going steady with you for three weeks but I think we should call it off. Even if it's a great personal loss to both of us, I'm sure we'll walk away stronger and nobler. Yours sincerely, Nick."

I slipped the letter to her in Computers. She didn't take it too badly, just ripped it up and fed it through the shredder. But then two days later photocopies of my *personal* letter started to circulate the school.

I didn't mind, though, because as a result of that, Goggle-eyes Gilda slipped me a note in History that said, briefly: "I like your style, Nick. You've got depth." I took another look at Goggle-eyes. I didn't mind her style either. She has this terrific laugh and she's a whiz on computers.

I wrote back straight away, my own kind of letter this time—honest and to the point: "Dear Gilda, That three-minute talk you gave on speech day about Third World Famine Relief was really excellent. I'll be eating lunch in the quad if you'd care to join me."

I Remember Gloria

Norman Marks

Gloria was a human doll.

In 1946 I was fourteen, with the longest arms and legs in the world and hair that never stayed flat. I stumbled a lot. I bumped into things. I dropped things. I was sure that everyone laughed at me as I went by.

But Gloria was a perfect doll. Doll's blonde golden hair. Doll's impossible blue eyes. Doll's perfect body. The light, flawless skin of a doll. Even a doll voice.

In my school there were other imperfect male human beings like me. We called ourselves "kids". We compared skin eruptions, erections and football cards. We practised telling dirty stories, farting and fumbling girls. Girls were almost as human as we were. Not as gross, not as imperfect, but approachable, touchable. They even seemed to be interested in us as the other sex. But Gloria was different.

Gloria appeared in our world one summer morning. School had resumed after the Christmas holiday and, still sun-peeling and water-logged, we sat in our familiar, changeless classroom, gazing vacant-eyed at the brassy summer world outside. Mr Dash arrived at our door. Standing in ballerina pose behind him was Gloria. An apparition, an angel.

Dot Dash introduced her to our form master and French teacher, Froggy Lingford. "This is Gloria Gold."

Even the name was perfect. Not one boy watching even fingered himself. Well, maybe Swampy Marsh did, but he was the grossest boy in school. We sat entranced by her ethereal beauty. Even Dot Dash and Froggy Lingford were affected. They spoke softly and tried to smile. They attempted little jokes. Gloria stood there meekly, her lips bow-shaped and perfect, slightly parted.

Over the weeks that followed Gloria became the main topic of conversation. Every male within range of her looks was smitten. She was treated better than a princess. I guess we thought she was something between royalty and deity. We all made attempts to talk to her, we all tried valiantly to improve our looks. For weeks I walked in a pungent haze of Californian Poppy hair oil, with drops of it running down my face.

My best mate at this time was Donny Maurice. Donny was gifted. He could swim and play cricket and tennis with a natural grace that left the rest of us homemade athletes angry but admiring. To our surprise Gloria settled on Donny and me as the males she most liked to talk to. Her conversations, always conducted in that strange doll voice, left us depressed, confused and anxious. We felt the conversations lacked depth and purpose, and blamed our own stupidity, our crassness. We were sure that, given more experience, more maturity, our communication with Gloria would move from this vague, imperfect level to messages of great meaning and impact.

We had conversations like this:

"My mother thinks I should wear red ribbons in my hair always." Delivered in that one-note, doll voice.

"Red sure is your colour," from me, struggling to add a deeper, more significant meaning.

"My father hates red. He always wants me to wear blue."

"Jeez, blue goes with your eyes," I panted. Somehow, these less than intimate exchanges left me short of breath.

"Some days I wear red. Other days I think blue looks better."

"Yeah." What else could I say?

"I sometimes wish I had black hair like Amanda."

"No! No! Your hair is perfect. I'll bet it feels as good as it looks."

Despite these brave attempts, our relationship remained static. However, even in that endless summer, change was brewing. It was a Saturday. We had ridden our Speedwells and Malvern Stars to the swimming hole seven kilometres out of town. We had bought a packet of Log Cabin tobacco and some Tally Ho cigarette papers as a communal sinful enterprise.

There was me, Donny, Swampy, Jim Summers and Peter Burrell. We swam, climbed trees and puffed at long skinny cigarettes. We were squatting in waist-deep water, probably talking about girls, when "Shit! Look!" exploded Swampy, pointing to the bank. Sitting on our piles of discarded clothing were three girls. We knew them, of course: slightly older than we were and usually infinitely superior. But on this hot summer afternoon they sat on our clothes, looking down at us crouching in the water, and giggled and whispered.

"Go away," shouted Donny.

"Make us," they called back.

"Jeez, what'll we do?"

In the silence that followed we all felt the defenceless helplessness of being stark naked. Swampy spoke. "Let's rush 'em. Let's all stand up and run at 'em at the same time."

I thought of my peanut-sized penis snuggled between my legs and silently said, "Never."

"All right," said Donny, the ever brave. "After three. One. Two. Three."

In a flurry of water we were up and out of the swimming hole. To my surprise I was racing along with the others, sure that all eyes were on my wrinkled cock. As we scrabbled up the bank I saw to my relief that the girls were off and running. We arrived at the piles of clothing, grabbed our shorts and held them to cover our family jewels—all of us except Peter Burrell. Head down, arms pumping, Peter charged on mindlessly, ignoring cat-heads and bindy-eyes, his white bum stark against the brown of his body. Just as it seemed he must catch the girls, they arrived at their bikes and pedalled off with loud, breathless peals of laughter. Peter stood stock-still for some moments, then turned and trudged slowly back to us.

By the time he arrived we were adding the finishing touches to the story of how Peter, in the raw, had chased three girls. We established the story, gave Peter a speaking part and an erection. By Monday at school Peter would be a legend.

We cycled home late in the afternoon, Donny and I together behind the others.

"That's made me think," said Donny.

"What? Them sheilas?"

"Well, the whole thing."

"Whadd'ya mean?"

"Well, the way we chased them sheilas and the way Peter just kept after 'em."

We pedalled in silence.

"We both like Gloria. But we don't do nothing about it. Startin' Monday I reckon we ought to get after her properly."

"Howd'ya mean? Chase her?" I was confused.

"No." Donny was riding head up and smiling now. "But stop messing around, just talking to her."

As we rode over the brow of the hill and down into town his smile grew wider. "Got it. I'm gonna write her a proper love letter. My brother's got a book on writing letters to sheilas."

My heart sank. Competing with Donny was bad enough, but Donny armed with a book like that left me defeated. Why couldn't my brother own a book like that? We parted. Donny smiling and confident. Me frozen, defeated.

The next day I moped around the house until Dad, fed up with my sulking, ordered me to cut the lawn. I pushed the clattering old hand-mower savagely, cursing the spongy Kikuyu. My nineteen-year-old brother, whose curly hair always looked recently combed and brushed, stopped me just short of destroying the strawberry patch.

"What's wrong, mate?"

I loved and admired my big brother too much to lie, so I told him of my broken heart. He listened with care, as always, and when I had finished my sorry tale he smiled and said, "You don't need a book on letter writing. You're always writing poetry. Write her a love poem." He added the clincher, "Girls go crazy over love poems."

Here was ultimate experience speaking. Hadn't I seen him kissing Rosa O'Leary, the policeman's daughter? A kiss that lasted so long that it seemed they must both expire for lack of air? This, then, was real maturity speaking.

I retreated to my room, my heart pounding with poetic lust. Hours later my poem was completed.

Gloria has big blue eyes,
eyes as good as summer skies.
Gloria has such pretty hair,
for her I'll always really care.
When she smiles and speaks to me
I'd give anything her hero to be.
She's so lovely, she's so cute
All us boys just think she's beaut.
One day I'll do something really brave,
And my hungry lips she'll finally crave.

That Monday before school Donny showed me his letter. He was nervous and kept asking if the letter was too formal. I was encouraging, patronising. Then, just as we went to class, I told him that my poem to Gloria was ready for the final rewrite.

"Poem?" he said, stunned. "You wrote her a poem?"

"Yeah! They're easy to do." I was casually in control.

In class he whispered, "Can I see it?"

I passed the poem to him. He read it, sat quietly, then re-read it and finally passed it back.

Ever honest, he said, "That's good. That'll do it." I knew he was crushed.

By Wednesday the poem had been read by half the boys in school and most of the girls. One of the girls, Judy Hammond, even offered to do a neat printed copy for me. However, the group consensus was that it should be in the poet's own best handwriting.

Gloria knew all this and seemed impressed. Finally she asked, with raised eyebrows, "When do I see this poem?"

I gave it to her.

She read it.

Nothing.

She re-read it.

Still nothing.

Finally, "Walk me home after school."

The world was filled with bright, silvery light, and my breath burned in my throat. All I could do was nod wordlessly.

By 3.30 pm and final bell, every kid in the school knew Gloria and I were going together and I was to walk her home. My standing among the kids had gone from average to top spot.

I seemed to take forever to reach the school gate. Everyone stood around in small, quiet groups. Gloria waited, alone and serene. I walked to her and silently accepted her school bag. We walked off together. We crossed the War Memorial park and turned down Darling Street. I thought of saying something about how prophetic this was, and decided that a really mature man would find this too crass.

Gloria said, "We're in the right street . . . darling!"

"Yes. So true," I simpered.

We left Darling Street and turned into Bridge Street and walked until the footpath and river bank were only metres apart.

"Let's walk under the willows."

Even as she spoke we were turning towards their shelter.

Once under the willows, she rested a hand on my arm. I took her hand, conscious of my sweaty palms. Now the levee bank hid us from the road. We passed under a willow tree whose branches hung almost to the ground.

We stopped.

We faced each other.

I put her school bag down.

We stepped closer. Almost touching.

I remembered how Humphrey Bogart had held a girl as he kissed her in a movie we had seen the week before. I remembered my three previous attempts to kiss girls. The first had ended in near disaster with her nose against my lips, the second had resulted in a clash of teeth that left both the girl and me shaken and embarrassed. The last I had jerked away from just before contact as I was assaulted by her violently bad breath.

Gently I moved the last few centimetres.

Gently I slid my arm around her and took the back of her head in my left hand while my right encircled her waist.

Humphrey Bogart, I thought.

Gently my lips met hers.

Gently we moved against each other.

Gently but firmly our lips fused.

Total shock and horror followed.

I leaped back, startled, horrified, stung!

I backed off under the willows, aware of her startled gaze and wide-open mouth. I ran. As I ran over the levee bank and on to the footpath, I found most of the kids waiting.

"What happened?" asked Donny as I ran up. "What's wrong?"

I stopped, gasping for breath, unable to tell them of the horror that had befallen me. They grouped around, all asking questions until I finally found my voice.

"I was kissin' her and," I faltered, "and she stuck her tongue in me mouth."

Total silence. I was surrounded by kids as stunned as I was.

"Right in. She stuck it right in. I thought I was gonna chuck."

"What?" said Donny. "Are you sure? It must have been an accident."

We stared at each other, and he said, rather weakly, "Maybe she don't know any better."

Slowly we walked away to cricket practice. Subdued and baffled.

Swampy Marsh summed it up. "What a waste of a good poem. You can never tell about sheilas."

First Love

Geoff Goodfellow

I started looking for love at thirteen, when men were just starting to explore space. How scientists could put people up there but were unable to do anything for the bumps and craters that had started erupting on my face had me baffled. Life became a series of daily rituals: squeezing and pumping in front of the mirror, and hating myself for not being able to say no to the cream buns from the homemade cake shop where I worked part-time. The only consolation was that the ten bob I earned there each week did make it possible for me to get into the Saturday night dances, where I hoped to find that special someone.

For over three years I haunted The Palais, a dance hall that seemed as big as a football oval. It stood opposite the Royal Adelaide Hospital on North Terrace, and I always hoped that an off-duty nurse would sweep me into her arms and care for me.

Every Saturday night I'd be there. Always dressed in my skin-tight black strides, black shirt with the collar turned up, and shirt sleeves rolled so far up my arms they nearly became tourniquets. And I had the shoes too. Black pointy-toed boots that looked so sharp you'd swear they could cut. I reckon they hung over my toes by the width of a cigarette packet—but that came in handy occasionally, as the spikes of the girls' stiletto heels could just about drive through the jarrah floor.

And I had plenty up top in those days. Hair, I mean. Most young people did. But not just hair. It was Brylcreem for the boys, and hair-spray for the girls. My hair was worn swept back at the sides to a duck's-tail, with a tousled curl drooping over my forehead. It gleamed just like the hair of the bloke on the black-and-white telly who sang, "Brylcreem, a little dab will do you—Brylcreem, the girls will all pursue you." I would have liked to have met up with him and told him just how many girls had run the other way when they saw me coming.

While boys' hairdos were greasy, girls looked as though their hair had been fibreglassed into huge erect beehives. They certainly felt that way too—if you were lucky enough to get that close.

This was the era of bodgies and widgies and the police anti-larrikin squad. We had Elvis Presley, Bill Haley, Connie Stevens and a host of other Americans influencing our culture, and if you went to The Palais, you were a product of that influence. You probably came from the northern suburbs, the western suburbs or close to the city. And it was a certainty you were being groomed (or had been) at your local Tech for a factory job. The eastern and southern suburbs were more likely where your dad's bosses lived—and you "knew" things were different on that side of town. Their sons and daughters didn't go near The Palais. They were turned on by the Beach Boys and the alternative surfie culture. They came from the quiet side of town (except for around Edwardstown), and did the stomp rather than rock'n'roll—'cos you can't jive on the beach.

Back at The Palais, the car park was always chock-a-block with Ford Customlines, Chevvy Coupes, chopped and channelled FJ Holdens—and an assortment of empty bottles, regardless of the law that insisted that no alcohol be consumed within two hundred metres of a dance hall. If you drove an Austin A40, a Morris Minor or a Ford Prefect, you parked it a block away—or wore the insults. Motor bikes crowded the kerbs. Hundreds of them. Parked on 45-degree angles and dripping oil on to the bitumen: 650cc Triumph

Thunderbirds and BSA Gold Flashes, most of them with the baffles knocked out of their mufflers by a length of water pipe. Hearing them all start up in unison at midnight when the dance closed seemed a poor consolation for being under sixteen and not owning one. Especially knowing that a huge mob of them would be heading out with a convoy of V8s to the Burnside roundabout to flour bomb any of the surfies still hanging around the Princeton Club. That made you realise what being sixteen really meant.

I made it through those three years of rejections, eruptions and false starts, getting the occasional dance, but never staying long enough with anyone to be able to work out how to undo a bra with one hand.

I thought I was doomed.

Then The Palais closed, and only the KT Club in King William Street seemed to cater for the remnants of my culture. I tried it out, along with many others from the old haunt, but its nickname, "the kiddies and toddlers", soon turned us away.

Two months later I did fall in love, with a BSA 650 in a motor bike shop in Kilburn. Like all loves it was traumatic. But after a few scary days locating an agreeable guarantor and organising finance, my luck did start to change.

The Palais re-opened. A new venue had been located opposite the Adelaide Railway Station, on the first floor of what was then the Railways Institute. A flasher looking building than its previous home, with a wide, white marble staircase and central brass handrail leading on to North Terrace. And I'd met Kathy.

That had happened outside the fish-and-chip shop in O'Connell Street, North Adelaide, on the previous Thursday night. I was sitting on the bike eating two bob's worth of chips and trying to look tough when she appeared. She had just come downstairs from the 707 Club, an adjacent coffee lounge where they had live music, with her girlfriend, Jenny.

"Nice bike," she said. "I bet it flies."

I was a bit stunned, but jumped back with, "Hop on the back and find out—if you've got enough guts."

"I'm with my girlfriend, but if I wasn't, I would for sure."

"Here, she can finish these off," I said, leaning forward with the steamy newsprint package. "C'mon. Jump on and I'll give y' a quick spin around the block."

"Yeah, OK then," she said impulsively. "You don't mind, do you, Jenny?"

I could see from the look on Jenny's face that she did, but she nodded anyway.

"Won't be long, Jen," I said.

"Jenny it is. J-e-n-n-y. Jenny's my name, thank you."

Touchy bitch, I thought, kicking the bike in the guts. "Yeah, OK, Jenny. Sorry about that one. Hop on and hang on tight," I yelled.

Kathy loved it. Wheelstand and all. We were back within minutes and I could see from Jenny's resigned look that she was far from impressed. We finished off the chips together, then split, agreeing to meet out the front of The Palais just before eight o'clock on Saturday night.

I spent all Saturday afternoon polishing the bike. The alloy side plates, the chrome and the paintwork. I even got the boot polish out and tidied up the saddlebags and tyres. It was gleaming.

I arrived about fifteen minutes early and backed the bike up to the kerb. The same 45-degree angle I'd seen at the old Palais—but the bikes just weren't around any more. The old culture had started to disintegrate. Everyone seemed to have grown up—either that or they'd got married or lost their licences. Whichever way, it all depended on a licence of some sort. Or maybe they'd been carted off to reform school or gaol. I sort of wanted to lose my freedom—but without some big heavy in a uniform standing over me and jangling a bunch of keys in my face. I was thinking about what Saturday nights might be like for those who were locked up when Kathy's voice surprised me.

"Hi Bluey, the bike looks fab," she said, moving towards me and leaving Jenny stranded in the middle of the footpath.

"Yeah. Gave it a quick tidy up this arvo." I leaned forward and pulled her towards me with my eyes, whispering, "I'll take y'home tonight eh?"

"Nah. I've come with Jenny, so I really should go home with her."

I was thinking about how I could change that when I yelled, "Watch this," and kicked the bike into action. I pulled out on to North Terrace, spun the bike around and mounted the footpath. The crowd scattered. I headed up the stairway, bouncing from step to step. I'd counted about five thumps from the back wheel when a blond-haired bouncer with a crew cut started to leap down from the foyer, three steps at a time. I backed off the throttle and let the bike roll back on to the footpath, lucky to have kept it upright. All the heads that had been peering up the stairway drew back, startled. I dipped the clutch, fed in the revs and screamed back over the kerb on to the roadway. Old bullneck stood there waving his big meaty fist in the air and yelling as I fled down the road. I waited for about five minutes for him to do a disappearing act before I returned to park the bike and catch up with the girls.

"You're mad, Bluey. Bloody crazy. He would've killed you if he got his hands on you," Kathy said.

"Well, he didn't, and he probably won't. Goin' up?" I pointed.

"Yeah, orright," Kathy said. "But do y' reckon it's safe?"

"Only one way to find out," I said.

The three of us found a table together and settled in for the night. I had a few dances with Kathy, but she always seemed to be disappearing and then suddenly re-appearing on the dance floor with some other lad. I wondered what her game was, but after three years of virtual solitude I decided to go along with it. I spent most of the evening talking to Jenny, just small talk, but I found she wasn't the shy girl I first picked her to be.

After the last dance I knew I'd be going home alone. But I thought I might be able to set something up for the following week with the three of us and my mate Wally.

"Listen. How'd it be if I got me mate to come next week? I'll borrow me old man's car and the four of us could come here together. We'd pick y's up and that."

They both agreed, and I was sure Wally wouldn't mind.

As I was easing out the clutch to leave, Kathy said, "You better not pick us up from home, 'cos me mum's real strict. We'll meet y's on the corner of Prospect Road and Regency—'bout half past seven."

"No worries," I yelled. I gunned the bike along North Terrace, over-revving it as I changed back through the gears to make the hollow boxes cackle.

Wally thought it was a great idea when I put it to him. We both agreed that seeing we always got about in jeans, jackets and flying boots—because of the bikes—we'd wear suits. We thought it'd blow the girls out a bit. There was another reason: I seldom got the chance to borrow the car, especially after I'd forgotten to re-connect the speedo cable one night and got sprung by the old man. If he knew we were both going out dressed up in suits, we'd have a much better chance of scoring the EK for the night.

The girls were waiting on the corner when we arrived. Wally had bought a bottle of muscat on the way, and by the time I'd parked the car there was only a dribble left. The girls both had a bit of a charge but Wally had done most of the damage. He was a bit nervous about a blind date and thought the alcohol would relax him. I'd told him that Jenny looked pretty good in black tights and filled her blouse out really well, but he was up-tight about having to dance. Just before buying the bottle he'd said to me, "What d'y' reckon, Blue? Like, I know I'm no Elvis with the hip-swivelling caper. Do y' reckon she'll give me a hard time or what?"

"You'll be laughin', Wally. Laughin', man. Just relax, eh, and do y' best."

He was far from laughing, though. The muscat relaxed him all right. He didn't dance, didn't even talk—just sat there.

Kathy and I danced together till the first break, when I headed off to buy a round of Cokes. When I returned, Kathy's chair was empty. Wally was nearly asleep, and Jenny was sitting there, chin in hand.

"Where's Kathy?" I asked.

"Oh, she's over talking to Tony . . . She'll probably be back in a minute."

"Had a dance yet, Jenny?" I enquired.

"No, not yet," she said glumly, looking at Wally.

"I've gotta go to the toilet," Wally said, excusing himself.

Jenny and I sat there together, sipping Coke and talking about our respective jobs. She was a checkout operator and hated it. I was a steel-fixer and loved it—so she did most of the listening.

The band started playing again, and Kathy still hadn't returned. I looked across to where she and Tony had been talking, but they weren't there. Then I spotted them on the dance floor, wrapped around each other.

"What's her game, Jenny?" I asked angrily.

"Ah, I dunno. She's always like that. Likes leading boys on—then gives 'em a hard time. She's funny like that."

"Bloody hilarious," I replied. I sat there fuming, staring at her untouched bottle of Coke and bouncing the straw around.

I looked Jenny over again. I was thinking—she's really very pretty. I wonder . . .

I cleared my throat and said bravely, "Hey Jenny, how

about a dance with me?"

"OK then, Bluey. Can't see why not—two can play her game."

The band was playing a slow ballad, Roy Orbison's "Pretty Woman". It seemed appropriate. As the light bounced off the revolving mirror ball, we floated into each other's arms, and I felt a slow tingle run the length of my spine. I hadn't felt that sensation before. It seemed incredible . . . And it was recurring.

The Flea

Peter McFarlane

It wasn't as if Cesare didn't take out girls. He did. He'd been taking them out for ages. He and Jaime had started taking them out every Friday or Saturday night for over a year now. They'd begun to wonder what they did with their time before.

And it wasn't as if he hadn't had sexual experience before. He had. He'd had it with some of the girls he'd taken out. And he and Jaime talked about sex all the time when they got together, so he knew all about girls.

Girls liked Cesare. They thought he was cool, and they reckoned he had a sweet nature, but they liked Jaime more. Whenever Jaime came into a room, girls always called out to him. He was tall and blond and dressed up a bit. But it wasn't that, or his reflecto sunglasses, or his earring; and it wasn't that the girls were usually younger than he was: he had sex appeal. He was a spunk. Girls loved him. And he loved girls; and he took out lots, and they all looked up at him with adoring eyes and told him he was wonderful. They said nice things to Cesare too, but nothing like the things they said to Jaime. Often he and Cesare took turns borrowing their parents' cars, and together they took out girls to parties or discos, or to the drive-in. After they'd taken them out, they spent all their time talking about them and what they'd done.

When Cesare and Jaime took out the same girl, they compared notes. They learned a lot from each other. Often Cesare took out girls after Jaime had finished with them. That didn't matter to Jaime. He didn't think he owned them like some of the other boys did. He was still interested in what happened with Cesare, and was never surprised or upset, even if Cesare did things Jaime didn't. He liked it when

Cesare did well. It was as if they'd been on a holiday to the same place at different times and he wanted to know what the weather had been like when Cesare was there. If it was really good, Jaime often went back again.

Cesare didn't mind. He made jokes about it. "Hey, Jaime," he'd say, "I only gave Kylie a three-star rating; you're acting as if she's a five-star resort!"

None of the girls seemed to mind, either. Some of them even joined in, joking how they'd have to try to improve their rating. "When are you going to take me out again, Jaime? I've been saving myself up," they'd say.

The girls in their own class were different. They were the same age and more like mates or sisters. Most of them had gone out with older boys when they'd been younger, and they enjoyed hearing about Jaime's and Cesare's adventures. Tania was one of them.

Jaime had decided long ago that Tania was the best-looking girl he knew, and Cesare agreed with him. When he and Jaime went down their list of girls, they both said Tania was the best. It wasn't just that Jaime said it. Sure, that made it definite, gave it an official seal, like when they announced the winner in the Academy Awards on TV; no, Cesare thought it too. Tania was intelligent and beautiful and great to be with, and they looked forward to seeing her at school. Neither of them thought of asking her out, because she had an older boyfriend who worked and had his own car, not just his parents' with "P" plates on it. Besides, they enjoyed the adoration of the younger girls.

If Tania had given them the come-on, it would have been different. But she didn't, even when they talked about the most intimate things. Once, when Tania hinted at what she did with her boyfriend, Cesare couldn't think straight. "Of course, he's demanding sexually," she said, "but I don't mind. I like it." Statements like that in French lessons drained French vocabulary from his head and made him feel he was in the dressing-room of a film star rather than in a cold, colourless classroom with an old fogey of a teacher and half-interested kids. But Cesare never considered asking her out. In her case he was an excited observer, not a participant.

"The Flea" changed everything. It was Tania who told Cesare about it. "The Flea" was a poem by John Donne. Her boyfriend had shown it to her. She said he'd studied it in English and had had to write essays on it. It was all about a flea that joined two lovers together by sucking their blood. Cesare didn't understand it at first, but when Tania read it out loud, he found himself blushing with excitement, particularly when she said the bit about sucking:

It suck'd me first, and now sucks thee,
And in this flea, our two bloods mingled bee.

She told him the poet was getting the girl to come across, but she said the girl didn't need too much convincing; she was enjoying it as much as he was. Tania read the poem again, but when she got to the end and said the words, "when thou yeeld'st to me", instead of just reading them and laughing as if she was talking about other people, she looked Cesare in the eyes and made it clear she was thinking of him; she wanted him to yield to her.

Cesare felt himself melt under her gaze. He understood how girls felt when rock stars picked them out of screaming audiences at concerts and got them up on the stage. He knew he was hooked. Tania was calling him, and he was giving himself to her. He'd never felt so excited. Suddenly he was out of control, a slave to Tania's wishes. He realised with a shock of recognition that this was what people felt when they were in love. He, Cesare, was in love!

He didn't tell Jaime. It wasn't that he was worried Jaime might muscle in. No, he didn't tell Jaime because he was in love and didn't want to talk about Tania in the same way as they talked about the other girls. Worse still, he was in love with a girl who was going out with someone else. He had no guarantee she was in love with him and he felt a bit foolish.

It was easy to avoid seeing Tania's boyfriend. So that she could study, Tania's parents made it a rule she wasn't to go out during the week, and that meant her boyfriend saw her only on weekends. If her parents thought Cesare was helping her with her schoolwork, he could go around any time. Tania encouraged him to, and because her mother was always very welcoming, Cesare found himself going around to her house all the time. Tania told him her parents were worried about how serious she was getting with her boyfriend, and they liked it when she was with people her own age. Cesare liked her parents, but he wondered if they would be as friendly towards him if they knew he was in love with their daughter.

Tania's mother asked him for Italian recipes. Cesare said he didn't cook, but she persisted. "I know how you Italian boys are looked after by your mums," she said. "See if you can get some of her favourite recipes, and then I'll spoil everyone with some yummy Italian cooking. You can stay on if you like and make sure I cook it right."

Cesare jumped at the invitation, bringing some of his mum's recipes for Tania's mother, and, tucked away in a bag to read to her later, a book of John Donne's poems for Tania.

He'd found the book in the library and read some of the love poems in it. He didn't think they were as good as "The Flea". Some of them had big words and bits that were spelt funny, but he found lots that described just how he felt:

If yet I have not all thy love,
Deare, I shall never have it all . . .

and

For every houre that thou wilt spare mee now,
 I will allow,
Usurious God of Love, twenty to thee . . .

He'd had to look up "usurious", but once he'd worked out it meant the god of love was like a banker who would take twenty of his hours to her one, he thought it was just right. He didn't understand the rest of the poem, or many of the others, but he kept finding bits that made sense:

Oh doe not die, for I shall hate
All women so, when thou art gone . . .

He couldn't wait to get inside Tania's room to read them all. With any luck Tania would read "The Flea" to him again.

It didn't take long for Jaime to find out that Cesare was seeing Tania. He knew something had happened when Cesare said he wasn't going out with anyone on the weekend.

"What's wrong?" he asked.

"Nothing."

"What are you goin' to do on the weekend, then?"

"Nothing."

After he asked around a bit, Jaime soon worked it out. "You're taking Tania out, aren't you?"

"No."

"I don't believe you. You're seeing her all the time."

"She's got a boyfriend, you know that."

"Well," Jaime said, becoming more curious, "what are you doing with her? You're spending all your time up at her place."

"I help her with English and stuff."

"You help her!" Jaime said with a laugh. "She'd be more likely to help you, you whacker."

Jaime wasn't convinced, but he didn't ask any more questions. Cesare was relieved he'd let it drop. He didn't want to tell him all they did was listen to records and read poetry. It would have been hard to explain how exciting it was having Tania read John Donne's love poems to him in her bedroom; how it was better than looking through porno magazines at the newsagents; and how he'd listen to her and dream that the poems she read were written about them. "Look at this one," she'd say. "This one's about two lovers lying in bed in the morning. They've been together all night and the man is angry at the sun for shining through the window and ending their lovemaking." It was hard to tell Jaime how, as she had read the opening of the poem, he'd imagined he was the lover in bed with Tania, and the sun outside was the one in the poem.

> *Busie old foole, unruly Sunne,*
> *Why dost thou thus,*
> *Through windowes, and through curtaines call on us?*

Although just listening to Tania reading these poems was exciting, Cesare felt sure she wanted more from him. But even though he'd been out with lots of girls, he felt a novice with Tania and didn't know where to start. His main worry was that he would make a move and she would reject him. The fear of this rejection held him back. He would have been distraught if Tania had said he couldn't see her any more and didn't let him into her bedroom. When they'd been mates he'd found it really easy to be intimate with her; now that he was intimate with her he felt awkward and uneasy about touching her.

"The Flea" changed everything again. One evening, a few weeks later, Jaime and Cesare were together when Jaime suddenly slapped his leg, leaving a bright red smear on his skin. "Man, this mosquito's had a feed," he said, adding with a wry smile as he changed the words to fit, "'It suck'd *thee* first, and now sucks *me*, /And in this flea, our two bloods mingled bee.'"

Cesare was shocked. The first time he had heard those words he had blushed and felt breathless with excitement. Now he felt battered and betrayed. He was speechless. He didn't want to ask Jaime how he'd heard the poem because he already knew the answer. Jaime understood his silence and explained. "Tania told me."

"When? I've been round at her place almost every day. When did you see her?"

"I took her out last weekend."

"What about her boyfriend?"

Jaime smiled in his confident way, as if it was perfectly natural they should break up now he was on the scene. "They've split up. Tania said she's been wanting to do it for some time. She said she only stayed with him because her parents were trying to break them up."

Cesare started to understand why her parents had made such a fuss of him. He began to wonder whether Tania really liked him or whether she had put it all on. "Are you taking her out again?"

"Oh yeah. Tania and I are going steady. I've decided to settle down. Tania's really keen, so I'll give the others a miss for a while. From the way she came on in the car on Saturday night," he added, leaning back in his chair, "I'm not going to miss them one little bit."

Jealousy overwhelmed Cesare. He felt sick in the stomach. He didn't know how he could tolerate the two of them together. As he looked at Jaime he imagined Tania touching him, and loving him. All the fragments from the poems that had meant so much to him were like little bits of paper he'd torn up and thrown into the air. Obviously they weren't special to Tania because she'd said them to Jaime. He began to torment himself by imagining Tania whispering them to Jaime in her bedroom.

"Why didn't you tell me you were going out with Jaime?" he asked when he saw Tania next.

"You didn't ask," she answered innocently.

Cesare realised there was no reason why she shouldn't go out with Jaime. He and she hadn't been going together or anything. If he had asked her to go out instead of dreaming of something magical happening between them, she might have gone out with him as well, he realised. He cursed himself for his lost opportunities. He had had his chance and had done nothing about it. The good thing was that he hadn't lost anything. He hadn't been rejected by her. He could still go on being her friend. He didn't want to read John Donne's poetry any more, but he knew they could still muck around the way they used to. It wasn't as if she was going to die or go away. She would still be his friend. He could still go to her place and her parents would still be as welcoming. And as Jaime was his friend, he'd still see a lot of her. Maybe Jaime would split from her, the way he always did with girls, and, when he did, he, Cesare, would still be around to pick up the pieces. He started to feel better.

As the weeks passed it became clear that Jaime and Tania were not going to break up. They became inseparable. Cesare felt very much on the outer as Tania and Jaime became passionate lovers.

Jaime's harem didn't seem to mind. The younger girls said how lovely it was to see them in love, and secretly hoped Jaime would be as loving and passionate towards them when he had finished with Tania.

Cesare knew it would be a while before that happened, if it happened at all. Jaime was a different person. He didn't seem to see other girls. He spent all his time with Tania in her room, in his parents' car, or in their favourite sleeping spot in the park at the end of her street before he took her home at night. Jaime and Tania were open about what they did together, telling Cesare about some of the funny things that happened. Jaime told him how one night he'd flattened the battery on his father's car and missed out on his regular lovemaking in the park. Jaime felt it was his right, a ritual he and Tania had to go through, and he determined to make up for it in some way.

His chance came when Tania's parents went to the movies. He and Tania pretended to leave early and then hid around the back until her parents had gone, sneaking in through the back door and spending the evening together in the empty house. It all went horribly wrong when they both fell asleep and were woken by the lights of her parents' car in the drive. Jaime grabbed his clothes, but Tania's father caught him climbing out of Tania's bedroom window.

Tania was grounded, and Jaime was banished from the house. As far as Tania's parents were concerned it was over between Jaime and their daughter. They couldn't keep them apart at school, but they could make sure Jaime didn't have anything to do with Tania afterwards.

For a moment Cesare wondered whether he would be able to have another go at taking Tania out, but as soon as he saw the effect of the separation on Jaime and Tania, he knew it would be hopeless. They became even more passionate and public in their displays of love for each other. Teachers tried to break them up in the schoolyard, but they just moved away to another place, and after a while even the teachers gave up and just scowled in their direction when they came upon them.

Eventually Jaime came to Cesare for help. "Look mate, I need a favour."

"Sure."

"I need you to take Tania out."

Cesare was puzzled.

Jaime went on. "I need you to take her out for me," he said. "We're going crazy. If we can't get to see each other we'll run away or something. All you have to do is pretend you're taking her out and bring her around to my place, and I'll do the rest."

"But won't her parents be suspicious?"

"Nah. You used to go around there a lot before. They'll think she's seen the light and wants to go out with someone decent for a change. All you have to do is start going around there after school and helping her with her English again."

Cesare felt a bit foolish. He'd tried to forget his infatuation with Tania, and Jaime was reminding him of it. Going around to Tania's house again would reawaken all those old feelings. However, there was no question what he would do. Jaime was his friend and he would help him.

It wasn't as bad as Cesare thought it was going to be. Tania was just as friendly as she had always been, and her mother was pleased to see him again. When she knew he was coming back, she made an Italian dessert for him to try. Cesare knew she was encouraging him to try to get Tania to forget Jaime, but she was obviously pleased to see him as well. Cesare liked the dessert, and when he came back a couple of nights later he brought her some of his mother's pickled eggplant.

They waited a week, and then, when both Jaime and Cesare knew they could get their parents' cars, Tania asked her parents if Cesare could take her out. "Lovely," her mother said, smiling at Cesare. "And where are you going to go?"

Cesare hadn't thought that far and was taken off guard. Tania covered for him. "We're going to the movies, Mum. There's a good movie on in town we both want to see."

"Lovely," she repeated. "I hope you have a really good time."

Both Tania's parents were at home when Cesare came to collect her. Her mother was relaxed as usual, but her father seemed a bit tense. He still hadn't got over the picture of Jaime, nearly naked, climbing out of his daughter's window, and he regarded all boys with suspicion.

On the way to Jaime's house Tania spoke. "It's like the poem, isn't it?"

"What do you mean?"

"'The Flea'. It's like 'The Flea'. You're the flea and you've brought Jaime and me together and made us one. 'This flea is you and I, and this'," she quoted, "'Our mariage bed, and mariage temple is'."

Cesare dropped Tania off outside Jaime's house, where

Jaime was waiting in his parents' car. Tania kissed him on the cheek, shouted a hurried thanks, and was gone, leaving him alone in the car. He might have brought them together like the flea in the poem, but now that she was gone, he felt empty and alone. He had the awful feeling that, like the flea, he was the one who was going to suffer. And he felt sorry for Tania's mother. He liked her, and now that Tania was with Jaime, he felt guilty that he'd deceived her. But the worst feeling was not having Tania in the car with him. In order to bring himself to collect her, he had kidded himself that he was really taking her out, even though he knew she was going to Jaime, and, as a result, he had revived all his old feelings of love for her. Now that she was gone he felt deserted.

As he drove the car back into the driveway of his house, he knew he wouldn't be able to take her out again. It made him feel too bad. He decided to tell Jaime that that was it. He wouldn't do it again. Jaime would kick up, he knew, and Tania might turn on her charms, but he was determined to resist them.

As it turned out, he didn't have to worry. Tania's father waited at the end of the street and caught Tania getting out of Jaime's car in the park. He marched them back to the house and got them to confess to the whole deception. Jaime told Cesare all about it the next day. "'Sfunny," he said with a strange smile, "he wasn't really angry at us. Because we're in love and all that stuff, he said we could keep on seeing each other. No, it was you he was angry at, mate. He called you all sorts of names and said he and Tania's mum would never trust you again. People are crazy sometimes, aren't they?"

The Black-and-White Boy

Gillian Rubinstein

"Cigareets and whisky and wild, wild women," the boy sang ironically. "They drive you crazy, they drive you insane!" Then he whistled appreciatively at Alison as she walked past him. You would think she hadn't noticed him from the way her head was turned scornfully away, but in fact she was acutely aware of every single part of him.

She had often seen him before. He was one of the youths who hung about, outside the shop, down the gravel pits, at the speedway. She had noticed the thick black hair, brilliantined in the current English fifties style, the chunky body that made him seem shorter than he really was, and something about the shape of his brow and his nose that made her think of animals.

She had been noticing him for months, appraising him for the honour of being Alison Fairlie's first love, but now that he had suddenly started to notice her back, she decided against him: too old (nineteen at least, when she was only fourteen); too *common* was what her mother would have said, but Alison, hating the word and all its connotations, substituted *available* . . . too . . . Free of him, she ran over the road to the shop, bought her mother's packet of Dunhill, and walked home again, daydreaming.

She wanted to fall in love, but she wanted it to be special. She wanted to create a first love for herself, in some way, that she could keep as a treasured memory for ever. It did not have to end in marriage, like fairy stories, or death, like *Romeo and Juliet*, but it had to be perfect. She kept a sharp eye out for her first love, without having any preconceived ideas about who it would be.

The boy outside the shop had only just started to notice her. Almost overnight Alison had turned into the sort of person whom men noticed. They put on their parading stance and preened themselves before her. Friends of her father sat next to her when they came to dinner, and paid her compliments. One or two of them kissed her on the lips. Their lips were surprisingly soft in their bony, bristly faces, and they smelled of after-shave and beer and tobacco.

Between her firm smoothness and their weathered skin lay her pity, curious and puzzled. She wondered what they wanted; they seemed satisfied with so little. Her eyes lost their childish clarity and became opaque like polished pebbles.

Alison often studied herself in the mirror, trying to glimpse what others saw. How did you know that you were pretty? No one ever told you outright, for fear of spoiling you and making you vain. You had to deduce it from negative information—the jealousy of other girls, your sister included; your mother's watchful anxiety; and the new, unmistakable, heady reactions of men.

The mirror showed her a serious person with a mass of wavy hair that was almost red, almost blonde, but not quite either, and eyes that were curiously almost the same colour. She was used to people saying, "What lovely hair!" They had been saying it all her life. What she heard was, "The rest of her doesn't add up to much, but the hair is lovely!"

"Would you call my eyes sloe shaped?" she asked her sister.

"I suppose so," Madeleine replied rather grudgingly. She had always been the pretty one up till now. She was sixteen and had a real boyfriend, a steady one, whom she had met at a Christmas party the year before. He wrote her letters from school, and took her to the cinema in the holidays. His people kept horses and Madeleine went to stay on their farm. He was seventeen, fair and big-boned. Alison tried to imagine what it would be like to be kissed by him. She made half-hearted attempts to win him away from Madeleine, but he saw her as still a child and treated her like one.

So you had power over some men, but not over all. How did you discern which ones? Did you wait to be approached, or did you go after them?

Alison's breasts grew. They were soft and lemon-shaped and they made her feel different, softened from the stick-thin tomboy she had been as a child. She became dreamy and distracted. Her mother noticed all these developments with alarm, and sent her to boarding school.

At school she missed the presence of men. How would she find her first love so far from them? She read love stories disguised in brown paper covers. She found herself wandering near the gardeners as they planted out dahlias and chrysanthemums. One of them, a boy straight out of school, asked her if she was courting, giving her bold looks from under lashes that lay thick and dark against a cheek brown from the outdoors, and slightly flushed. There was a hollow just below the eye socket which she longed to touch with inquisitive gentleness.

Girls, away from both men and mother, formed intimate friendships with each other. If these were across age groups they were called courting couples—CCs. On Sunday evenings CCs walked together on the playing fields and through the grounds. They held hands, kissed, touched, often wept.

The Latin teacher fell in love with one of the sixth form, and ran hastily out of the chapel one evening, her face ugly with controlled tears.

Alison watched them, aloof. She was slightly attracted to an older girl with boyish broad shoulders and cropped hair. She blushed when this girl came near her, and felt a sweet and exciting yearning that was for no one object and sought no particular form of expression. It existed, and it made her exist also. But she did not want this to be entered in her memory scrapbook as her first love.

She dreamed at night that she was cats, both male and female, driven desperately to couple, and the marvellous throb of sex wakened her. She lay in the darkened dormitory, amazed at her body's knowledge and skill, listening to the sounds of sleeping girls around her.

In the winter holidays Alison and Madeleine went as they always did to spend two weeks with their aunt and uncle, while their parents went away. There were cousins, Penny, just older than Madeleine, and Richard, just younger than Alison. Up till now, Alison had counted Richard as one of her best friends. They had always been a pair, as Penny and Madeleine had. But Richard was also aware of the change that had taken place in Alison, and she found herself isolated as she had never been before. The older girls talked about boys and clothes, and teased her. Richard disappeared all day.

Parties and dances were arranged for the young people. Alison unwillingly put on dresses of shot material that revealed her shoulders and throat and danced with young men in suits and cummerbunds. Sometimes they held her close in the last dance, and she felt their hardness against her, and her own answering desire. Often she trembled. But none of them aroused in her the tenderness that made her long to reach out to them and touch them. She ran away, sat in the Ladies' and read books, had to endure the mocking whispers of older girls.

In the village there was a youth club of sorts run by the garage owner, Eddy, a childless man in his early thirties, bored by marriage and sorry for the teenagers who had nothing to do in that remote area. Richard, in flight from what his class and upbringing had in store for him, spent his time with Eddy and the other kids, adopted their speech and dress, strove for their acceptance. Bored by the older girls and scornful of the young men in cummerbunds, Alison went with him.

There was a handful of boys, farm labourers' and smallholders' sons, and two or three girls whose main ambition was to be someone's girlfriend. They went to the river or to the beach, went to the nearest big town to the pictures or bowling, all piled into the back of Eddy's Land Rover, sitting on sleeping bags or rugs or on each other's knees. Eddy teased them, told them dirty jokes, flirted with the girls, wrestled with the boys, pointed out used french letters among the jetsam on the shore, gave them all the sex education they ever got. Parents disapproved of him.

Alison studied the group warily. It was one of those times when she would have preferred to have been a boy, to have been one of them rather than to be put with the other girls who wanted to be someone's girlfriend. She did not think she wanted to be a girlfriend to any one of these boys.

Then one night she dreamed the cat dream again. It had become more specific. She had become only the female cat. The male cat was black and white, and in the dream it turned into a person, a boy from the youth club whose name was David.

She awoke with a sense of amazement, David all black and white in her consciousness, and for ever afterwards the time with David would be black and white in her memory. Black hair and white, white skin, white wrists between the sleeves of the donkey jacket and the black leather gloves. White face, seen mostly at night and on dull, colourless winter days.

His name was David Barnes, but the others called him Basher. It was dangerous to call him that. He did not like it, but it was what he was. Eddy treated him with wary gentleness, defused his violence. David did not say much, but when he was relaxed, he sang in the back of the Land Rover, censored snatches of "Eskimo Nell" and "The Foggy, Foggy Dew"; the current pop hits, "Wake up Little Suzy" and "The Rock Island Line"; and then, surprisingly, old ballads, "Lord Randall" and "Green Grow the Rushes-O".

Here he is, Alison said firmly to herself. But what happens now? Both she and the black-and-white boy did nothing for a few days, but they watched each other when the other was not looking.

Penny and Madeleine joined the group one day to go to the river, adding a new and more daring element to it. The local girls wore high heels and tight skirts. Penny, Madeleine and Alison wore jeans and gumboots, and Penny and Madeleine practised their flirting on the boys. It was as though there were three sexes: boys, girls, and in-betweens who combined the seductiveness of the girls with the freedom of the boys. It made Alison feel happy and bold. When a mud fight started, she was in the thick of it. David was holding Richard in a half-nelson. She flew to them, partly to rescue Richard, partly to get close to David and touch him.

David laughed at her, holding her off with no trouble at all. His hands clasped her wrists as if they were sticks, white hands against her sallow skin, the nails broken and black. Then he turned her round as if they were dancing, and held her tight against his chest. For a moment their bodies rested against each other, recognised each other's longing for the easement of loneliness, and acquiesced. Then Alison dropped her head and bit him, not hard, at the base of his thumb.

His flesh tasted of salt and mud. The taste was in her mouth. The strength of her desire terrified her. He let go of her at once, and turned to pursue Richard.

On the way home, Madeleine sat next to David and tried to get him to sing. One of the other boys, Kenny, leaned over. "You're wasting your time. It's not you he likes, it's your sister."

"Belt up, you stupid git!" David said in the darkness, but he said it peacefully, for him, and he grinned across at Alison.

"Sing 'Once I had a secret love'," the irrepressible Kenny continued, and he started to warble it himself in a ludicrous parody. Alison hardly heard it. Her cheeks were on fire, and she was passionately thankful for the gloom in the back of the Land Rover. She couldn't stop grinning, and waves of happiness were flowing out from the pit of her stomach. They were the most beautiful words she had ever heard. "It's not you he likes, it's your sister." David did not like Madeleine. David liked Alison. And she liked him. Perhaps she even loved him. They had recognised each other in a magical way. Yes, it had to be love.

"Well, she doesn't like you!" Madeleine told David rather crossly.

"Yes, she does!" he replied confidently.

"You're pretty conceited, aren't you!"

He leaned forward so that their knees were almost touching. "You like me, don't you, Ali?"

Part of her was nearly fainting from the fact that he had used her name, part of her was longing to throw herself against him and feel his body against hers again; but another part of her, that she did not know existed, knew what to do. This new Alison tossed her head (*tossed my head? Me?*) and touched her lips with her tongue, and said "Like you? Don't flatter yourself!"

There was a chorus of mocking jeers from the boys, and giggles from the girls, and David, not in the least discouraged, let the swing of the vehicle jolt him forward so that their knees did touch. He put his hand out to steady himself, as if by accident, on her thigh. It felt as if an electric current had passed through her.

David left his hand there until Eddy stopped the Land Rover at the end of the cart track that led to the Barnes' farm. He gave her thigh one last, hardly noticeable squeeze before he hopped out of the back.

"Ta-ta!" he called to them all. "See you next time."

"You'll never guess," Penny said to her parents at dinner, and then proceeded to tell them. "Basher Barnes is soft on Alison!"

"Don't be silly," her mother said automatically. "Alison is too young for that sort of thing."

"I think Basher is rather sweet," Madeleine said wistfully. "But apparently he likes Ali!"

"You shouldn't call him Basher," Richard put in. "He doesn't like it."

"He is a bit of a basher, though, isn't he, Daddy?" Penny said.

"It runs in the family," her father commented. "The old man knocks the kids about a bit, and when David loses his temper, he does the same thing. The sort of person to stay away from, Alison. I'm sorry he's part of the youth club. I would have thought you could do without him there."

Alison said nothing. She thought of David. Now she felt sorry for him too. Her uncle and aunt did not approve of him. They thought he was violent. They thought she was too young for "that sort of thing". And, though they hadn't said so, she knew they would dismiss him as a "village boy", not the same class as they were, unthinkable as a boyfriend.

Snow fell that night, and lay fifteen centimetres deep by morning. It changed the everyday landscape into a different world in which all sorts of things became possible.

At the end of the day David came to the house, black hair white with snow, his breath a frosty cloud on the damp air. Alison, who had been waiting for him in some way all day, met him outside on the porch, before anyone else had a chance to see him.

"Eddy's taking us out tobogganing tonight. I wanted to know if you were going to be there," he said. He did not touch her or look at her. They stood a metre apart and spoke with great restraint as though nothing had happened between them.

"Suppose so," she said carelessly, in case she had imagined everything.

"I'll see you there, then."

His hands were shoved in the pockets of his donkey jacket, and he stamped his feet against the cold. The snow was blue-white in the gathering darkness, and when he walked away across the lawn, there were no other footprints in it but his.

The snow had stopped falling, and the moon had risen. It was freezing hard, and everything was black and white. Straightforward tobogganing down hill was too tame for Eddy. He tied two sledges on to the back of the Land Rover and drove in huge circles around the High Common, pulling the teenagers at forty kilometres an hour through drifts. The powdery snow flew into Alison's face, stinging her eyes and numbing her lips. Her hands turned to ice inside her soaked gloves, until she could hardly hold on to the sides of the sledge. David did not say a word to her, nor she to him, but every time it was her turn on the sledge, somehow it was his turn too, and he sat behind her and held on to her, and their bodies silently communicated with each other.

It was so exhilarating no one wanted to stop, and Eddy tuned in to their craziness and drove faster and faster, until Alison lost all sense of who she was and was aware only of the speed, and the snow, and the black night, and the stars, and the black-and-white boy.

David.

Eventually the Land Rover stalled in a huge drift, and they all tumbled off the sledges in a heap. That put an end to the tobogganing. Eddy could only get out of the drift in reverse, and by the time they had untied the sledges and helped push the vehicle free the magic was fading, and they all realised how freezing cold they were.

Alison sat shivering in the back of the Land Rover. David was sitting beside her. They still said nothing to each other, but his arm was stretched out behind her head. A few moments before she would have done anything for him, followed him anywhere, but that moment was past and she did not know how to retrieve it. She put her head back and let it rest on his arm, and he moved his arm very slightly so that he was holding her against his shoulder.

She would have liked him to hold her for ever, but five minutes later Eddy stopped at the end of the cart track, and David said "Ta-ta," drawing his hand across the back of her neck and holding her under her hair for a fraction of a second. Then he hopped out over the tailgate and staggered in the snow. "Cripes, I'm buggered!" he grinned, and thumped the back of the vehicle to tell Eddy he could go.

The snow flew up from the wheels as the Land Rover pulled away, and David waved goodbye, black against the white fields that stretched away on either side.

Alison never saw him again. The next day she and Madeleine went home, and soon the holidays were over. She went back to school and daydreamed about David's hand on her neck, and the taste of his skin in her mouth.

A whole term passed. Once again in the holidays Alison went to her uncle and aunt's. The youth club was no longer in existence. Eddy had left his wife and was living in a caravan with one of the girls who used to go to the club. She was already pregnant. People did not talk to them much, but Alison felt a strange loyalty to Eddy, and she wanted to hear about David. She walked up to visit them.

It was spring, damp and mild. The hedges were starred with yellow celandines and the elders around Eddy's caravan were putting out tiny furry leaves.

"Is David Barnes around?" she asked Eddy directly.

His dark eyes creased with knowing complicity. "You used to be a bit keen on him, didn't you?"

Alison shook her head, but smiled.

"He ran away from home," Eddy told her. "Right after that night we took the sledges out. His old man had told him not to go out with me any more, but you know Basher. He never took a blind bit of notice of anyone. The old chap gave him a hell of a belting when he got home, and the next morning young David had hopped it. His mother reckons he went to the coast and joined a ship, but no one's heard a thing from him."

Perfect, Alison thought as she went home. What a perfect thing to do, to run away to sea.

That was my first love, she thought, and it seemed to her as if she were carefully putting it away in a scrapbook like a photograph. A black-and-white photo of a black-and-white boy.

David.

She never forgot him.

How Do They Get Cranes on Top of Tall Buildings?

Doug MacLeod

I can make water!

All right, I know that most people can make water, but I can do it scientifically! I did it with the advanced chemistry set Mum and Dad gave me for my thirteenth birthday.

"Mind what you do, Brian," my dad warned. "We don't want you killing yourself after we spent all that money on your glasses."

Putting on those glasses that Dad was so worried about, I read the first experiment in the instruction book. It was a recipe for water—mixing hydrogen and oxygen. Making the hydrogen was easy but adding the oxygen turned out to be much more dangerous than the book let on. According to the book, you hold a lighted match over a test tube of hydrogen, and when you hear a popping noise you know that the oxygen has been added through combustion. The book made it seem very simple and there was even a picture of a serious boy, wearing a white coat and a Brylcreem hairdo, holding a match over his test tube. But pictures in science books are never true to life. It would have been far more accurate to show the boy with his hair standing on end, his white coat all mucky and his test tube completely obliterated. If only the picture had shown that, I would have been more careful. As it was, I held the lighted match over my hydrogen and there was a sonic boom. The bottom blew out of my test tube, terrifying my cat, IQ, and bringing my mother racing in from the back yard. Although I wrecked a perfectly good test tube and gave IQ the fright of his nine lives, water had been created. There was a little pool of it on the floor.

"Look at that!" I cried, showing Mum the pool.

"Brian Purvis," she moaned, "you certainly know how to scare a cat good and proper."

Yes, I'm clumsy. Everybody is clumsy now and then, it's just that I'm better at it than others. Like with food, for example. Eating dinner in front of the television is easy for most people, they just balance the plate on their lap. Me? I end up with dinner all over my pants. Plates just won't stay on my lap. I've got non-stick knees.

You could say I'm very attractive to accidents, which may be why I'm not so attractive to girls. They don't like clumsy guys who carry their books, then trip over and drop them down a stormwater drain. It's unromantic. It's uncool. It's also a waste of books. So I decided I was a bit of a no-hoper as far as girls are concerned. At thirteen, I was the only guy in my class who wasn't going out with a girl. All the guys had photos of their girlfriends, out-of-focus black-and-white prints which had been done in photography class and which had pride of place on the insides of locker doors. Me? I had the loneliest locker door ever. I was the lone brain, the sort who would grow into a mad scientist and spend his evenings building the perfect woman from bits of bodies and silicon chips. It was a frightening thought.

That was why I decided to fall in love with Julie Andrews. Not the Julie Andrews who was in *The Sound of Music* and *Mary Poppins* but the Julie Andrews who had red fuzzy hair and was in my class. Believe me, two Julie Andrewses could never be more unalike. While the film-star version was delicate and graceful, the red fuzzy-haired version was loud, rough and once boasted that she had smuggled a fairy penguin out of the zoo by stuffing it in her bag on a school excursion. She had no sense of humour, which in a way was a good thing because it meant that she didn't laugh at me all the time. Like most people, she called me Brain instead of Brian, but she seemed to respect me. At least, she always asked me if she could copy my answers in Maths.

"Julie wants to if you do," said Jim Conos.

Besides being Greek and good with girls, Jim thought it was his duty to arrange love affairs for other people. He wanted everybody to be as successful as he was, which was very unselfish of him and also got to be a pain in the neck.

"I'll take my time over it," I said.

"What do you mean, take your time over it?" Like his father, who was in the furniture business, Jim could be very persuasive. "We're talking about love, not TV sets. Make up your mind quick, or you'll spend all summer without a girl. Is that what you want? No girl for the holidays?"

"I'll speak with Julie this afternoon."

"Good. We got Science." Then he winked and added, "Chemistry—you know?"

He nudged me and there was a light jangling noise made by the many plastic bangles which he wore on his right arm. Those bangles were famous. Girls would buy them for him and Jim said that each one was like a victory to him. He had so many victory bangles on his right arm that I'll be surprised if it doesn't drag along the ground when he gets older.

"You want my advice?" he asked.

"Yeah. Sure."

"Don't give her your old line about how you can make water. It's not funny any more."

"What should I say?"

"Not your usual dumb stuff. Don't do Monty Python at her. Think of a good opening question." He frowned at me. "One she can answer."

So much for my question about how they get cranes to the tops of tall buildings.

Science classes in our school were unusual. Mr Lamb, our teacher, preferred art but taught Science only because there was a great shortage of Science teachers. This afternoon we were supposed to be investigating melting points, or how hot something has to be before it melts.

"Not everything melts at the same temperature," Mr Lamb announced, as if this was a fascinating piece of news that he had just discovered. Most people find this out very early in life when they notice that ice cream melts much more quickly than the cone it comes in, but Mr Lamb must have been a late developer. Or maybe nobody ever bought him ice cream.

"Repeat what I just said, Brian."

Mr Lamb's voice interrupted my thoughts of ice cream. I looked at him helplessly.

"Dreaming again," droned Mr Lamb. "What's the girl's name, then?"

He smiled as the class burst out laughing. Boy-girl jokes always got big laughs and Mr Lamb knew it and took advantage of it, just as Prep school teachers always tell toilet and underpants jokes to their kids on the last day of the school year. Everyone likes to be a comedian.

When the laughter had finished and Mr Lamb's moment of glory had passed, he went on to explain how we were to melt things over a bunsen burner. We were supposed to sift some powdered glass on to little pieces of copper, then hold them over the flame until the glass melted but the copper didn't, proving that glass has a lower melting point than copper. Amazing, eh? What we were really doing was using science as an excuse for making pretty enamel do-dads. If mine worked out, I decided I would give it to Julie.

Remembering what Jim Conos had said, I crept over to the bench where Julie was at work on her melting points. I had my opening question all ready.

"Do you know what the smelliest thing in the world is?"

Julie looked at me strangely and I thought for a moment she was going to yell, "You!", but her answer came after some thought.

"A baby. My sister's just had one."

"Boy or girl?"

"Girl. How come you asked me what the smelliest thing in the world is?"

"I just wondered if you'd be interested."

"You're weird, Purvis."

"No. You see, I invented it last night."

Julie was interested enough to keep talking so I figured that I was doing all right after such a shaky start.

"You invented what?"

"A stink bomb. An incredible stink bomb. It's phenomenal."

"A stink bomb?"

"I just thought, you know, with the end of the year coming up and everything, I just thought you'd like me to make you one."

"Hey!" squawked Julie.

Mr Lamb looked up from the art magazine he was reading at the front of the class, stared at us both, then continued reading.

"Hey!" Julie repeated softly. "A real stinkeroo, eh? How did you do it?"

"A table tennis ball . . ."

"Everybody knows that one."

"No, wait. A table tennis ball filled with some of my simple-to-make blue stuff."

Julie haphazardly sprinkled her copper pieces with glass powder. She was pretending to work.

"Do you light it? The stinkeroo, I mean."

"No. You pour a few drops of vinegar through a hole in the ball and it starts stinking."

"Good one, Brain. Good one."

It was exciting, discussing with Julie the possible uses of a Purvis stinkeroo. The library, the gym and the staff room would be good testing grounds. Julie wanted to put one in the boys' changing room and, though I felt like a traitor, I happily agreed that it would be a good idea. I had never seen Julie up this close before. She had lots of very pale freckles and she wore a bit of mascara.

"The class is nearly over," I said. "I better go and melt something."

"Promise to make me a dozen of your stinkeroos?"

"Sure." Then I said it. "Do you want to go to the pictures?"

I couldn't believe how cool I sounded.

"You mean like together?" said Julie.

I nodded.

"You mean like *going* together?"

"No. Not if you . . . yeah. Yeah. That's what I mean."

"Have you gone with many girls?" she asked.

"No."

"I didn't think so. You're not all that great looking."

She must have seen my face fall because she instantly added, "You're not bad, though. Not too bad. But you're clumsy. Plus you're a bit strange. Plus . . . you're on fire."

"Pardon me?"

"You're on fire! *Fire*, dummy!"

Julie was right. I had gone too close to the bunsen burner and touched it with the sleeve of the big baggy smock I was wearing. I cursed Mr Lamb for making us wear art smocks in Science class.

"I'm on fire!" I yelled.

"I already told you that," said Julie.

Mr Lamb put down his art magazine. When he saw my smouldering smock he didn't bother to make any silly comments. He just cried, "Roll! Roll on the floor, Purvis!" and ran over and tackled me. I rolled. Gradually, the flames went out. When I was sure I was no longer on fire, I stood up to a round of applause. I took a bow.

"You're an idiot, Purvis!" said Mr Lamb. "A flaming idiot."

The class burst out laughing. Once again, Mr Lamb was the stand-up comedian. He went on making jokes about my "burning love" for Julie Andrews and the "fire of my passion". Nothing could stop him. But I didn't mind because, after all that, Julie agreed to go to the pictures with me.

I arrived first at the cinema and bought us both tickets for a film which was supposed to be a comedy about a werewolf, Julie's choice, not mine. I took a quick look at myself in the floor-to-ceiling mirror, mainly to check that my fly wasn't undone, and suddenly noticed that I looked incredibly daggy. Brown jumper, brown pants, and my shirt collar was too wide. I felt even more gawky when Julie arrived wearing fashionably skintight jeans and enough mascara to polish a boot.

"Hi."

"Hi, Brain."

Now that we weren't at school, I had hoped she wouldn't call me that, but I didn't say anything. I felt awkward and I had a terrible feeling that I was about to do something daggy. In my mind I saw all the disastrous things that could happen, from losing the tickets to sitting on a melted ice cream in the cinema. A pity I didn't think about how lethal escalators can be.

We were taking the escalator to the second floor where the movie was showing. Neither of us was talking much. We didn't seem to have that much in common. Trying to be calm and cool, I rested a hand on the rubber rail of the escalator. Suddenly there was a screeching noise. A few people must have heard it because they stopped talking. The noise got louder. I discovered that my right foot was hurting and that I couldn't move it. I looked down. My trackshoe! The escalator was eating up my trackshoe! Somehow, I had wedged the rubber tip of my shoe between the step and the escalator wall. It was being chewed up. I curled my toes.

"What's that noise?"

Julie hadn't realised that I was in danger of losing a leg. I couldn't possibly let her know that I was so clumsy, so I pretended nothing had happened. I bluffed.

"Do you know how they get cranes on top of tall buildings?" I asked coolly.

Julie looked at me strangely, then noticed the game of tug-of-war I was playing with the machine.

"Your foot . . ."

At last I pulled my foot free, but not before the escalator had claimed the rubber toecap of a brand new trackshoe. My sock had a hole which my big toe poked out of. Julie didn't say a word. People everywhere were laughing; I even thought it was funny myself, in a way, but Julie was silent. I think she was embarrassed. That was when I realised her lack of a sense of humour wasn't such a good thing after all.

"Hey, Brain!"

It was a surprise to see Jim Conos at the top of the escalator, waving his bangled arm at us. At least, it was a surprise to me. He wore tight jeans and a red T-shirt which showed off his muscles as well as his bangles. Beside him was a dark girl who looked a little younger. I imagined this was his latest bangle-girl.

"This is a real coincidence," said Jim.

He flashed a look at Julie, who smiled back in a sort of way that made me think it wasn't such a coincidence after all.

"This is Mary," said Jim. "My sister."

It was more of an apology than an introduction.

"We should sit together, eh? Mary, you sit with Brain."

"Brain?" Mary looked surprised.

"Brian," I said.

Julie and Jim had obviously arranged to meet here and Mary was an unforeseen complication. As we moved into the cinema, Julie and Jim held hands. I felt numb. It took me a while to answer when Mary spoke to me.

"Are you a friend of Jim?" she asked.

"I think . . . yes," I said. "At school."

"I've seen you at school," she said, "but not very often with Jim."

"I spend a lot of time in the library."

"Yes. That's where I see you."

We handed our tickets over.

"I'm glad you're here," Mary said. "I wanted to talk to you in the library, but you always had your head down like you wanted to be alone."

"Why did you want to talk to me?"

"Just that . . ." Mary smiled and looked a bit embarrassed. "Just that you looked nice."

Jim and Julie were all over each other. It was terrible, sitting next to them in the back row and having to listen to their groaning snogging noises. To make matters worse, the film was so gory it was giving me a headache. I hated Julie and I hated Jim, though I knew Julie had never actually said she was going with me. And Jim had warned me to be quick, because getting a girlfriend wasn't like buying a TV set. Maybe I was just too slow about everything.

My headache got bigger and bigger. Finally I stormed out and went into the toilets. There I studied myself in the mirror to see if I actually looked sick. I was pale, but not really sickly looking. In fact, I was looking better and better as I stood there.

When I walked back out I saw Mary waiting there for me.

"Hi," I stammered. "I just needed to . . . you know."

"It's horrible, isn't it?" she said.

"The film? No, it's not even frightening." I looked at her and knew that I didn't have to pretend I was tough. "It's awful. Do you want to go somewhere else?" I asked.

We decided it would be nice to have coffee somewhere.

Sitting in the coffee shop, Mary and I talked about school. Then we talked about ourselves and found that we liked a lot of the same music, though she wasn't quite as mad about Uncanny XMen as I was. When I explained about my powerful stink bombs, Mary said it was a pity that we didn't have one back at the cinema to roll down the aisle.

The coffee arrived.

"I have to ask you an important question," said Mary, stirring the sugar in.

I kind of hoped she wasn't going to get all serious after we had only known each other for such a short time. But of course, I told her that she could ask me anything.

She took a sip of coffee. Perhaps she had decided not to ask me the question after all? But then she looked me right in the eye and said, "What I need to know is, what happened to the end of your shoe?"

I explained the whole business of the shoe-eating escalator and Mary laughed. She especially laughed when I told her about how hard it was pretending nothing was wrong.

"I know exactly what you mean," she said. "The same thing happened to me at my cousin's wedding."

"They had escalators there?"

"No, listen. It was very boring. All the grown-ups were making speeches in Greek. Jim and I got so bored, we started playing little games. We passed a bowl of tarama backwards and forwards under the table."

"Tarama?"

"Pink dip made from fish eggs," she explained. "We stuck in our fingers then put them in our mouths. The grown-ups didn't know we were doing it, though I got told off by Uncle Theo for sucking my thumb. Then Jim played a trick on me. He handed me a bowl of horseradish. Since it was under the table, I couldn't tell the difference. I scooped some into my mouth and it was burning hot, like mustard. I wanted to cry and scream but knew that I would get into trouble if I did, so I just sat there, gritting my teeth and staring at Jim as if nothing had happened. In the end it was Jim who got into trouble for bursting out giggling."

We talked for an hour or so, then realised that Jim and Julie had no idea where we were. We moved to go. When the waitress came to clear our table I noticed that there was nothing for her to clean. I hadn't spilt anything, not even one grain of sugar.

On our way back to the cinema, I thought it might look good if I held Mary's hand. Then I decided not to. Not yet, anyway.

I pointed out a new office block which towered over the old buildings and which was still being built.

"Do you know how they get cranes on top of tall buildings?" I asked.

"Piece by piece," said Mary. "One bit at a time."

First Impressions

Nette Hilton

Sometimes I just don't understand my mother. I mean, she shaves her legs. I know because there's at least 800 razors all over the bathroom and three in her make-up tray. I've even found one by the kitchen sink.

But—

"No," she said, "you don't need to shave your legs," and she went right on whisking the mashed potatoes. "Does she, Ron?"

"Mmmmmmmmm?" answered Dad. "No. Makes them prickly," and he went back to reading the newspaper.

"Anyway," Mum went on, "you're too young to be bothered about stuff like that. Plenty of time later on."

I took a deep breath. "Well, when can I shave them? Everyone else does."

"When you're sixteen." She didn't even hesitate. She practically smiled.

"Well, I'm not walking around like this"—and I poked my leg out—"until I'm sixteen."

"You'll be doing a lot of sitting down then."

Sometimes my mother thinks she is so smart.

"Hurry up and have a bath—dinner's nearly ready."

I mean, just like that, end of conversation.

I threw all my clothes in the middle of the bathroom floor and stomped on them. I looked in the mirror and then moved nearer to check the hair range. You know, how close you'd have to be before you saw the hairs. Definitely not close enough.

I stomped on my clothes again and swore all the swear words I know—including the "f" word.

"You in the water yet?"

"What?"

Nothing gets Mum going like "What?". I knew she wouldn't trek all the way down to check but I sloshed in anyway.

"Don't slop the floor, and pick up your uniform," yelled Mum. "You need it tomorrow."

How can someone two rooms away see all that and not understand about the hairs?

I grabbed a few in my fingers and pulled. Nothing happened. Tweezers should do it. I dripped over my uniform and tiptoed to the cupboard. There they were—about five pairs. Unreal. If my mother isn't shaving her armpits or her legs, she's plucking her eyebrows. I think she plucks little hairs out of her chin as well, but I'm not supposed to know that. I caught her once and she nearly ripped her chin off trying to cover up.

I propped my leg up and started tweezing. Do you know how many hairs there are on a leg? Absolutely millions. "God," I thought, "I'll be a hundred and four before I get all of them."

The razor blade grinned at me, but I was sure that if I used it Mum would know and ground me.

I really hated those hairs. I grabbed Dad's lump of pumice stone and attacked them. It hurt. It hurt a lot, but I didn't care. I'd show them. I went on scratching and scrubbing.

I was so busy I didn't even hear The Mouth come in.

"Mum said get washed and hurry up."

I threw the pumice stone at her. She grabbed it and ran. "Emmy being nasty. She threw a rock at me," she bawled. For a little kid she sure knows how to stir it up. I swear if Mum ever decides to have another one, I'm off.

"Out now!" Mum roared.

I stood on my uniform to get dry and checked the mirror

again. One leg looked pretty red but at least you couldn't see hairs. I moved closer. One leg definitely looked hairy. The other one looked red and blotchy and bare—in patches anyway. I couldn't get grounded for accidentally rubbing the hairs off. Good old pumice stone. I had to get it back. All I had to do was find out where The Mouth had dumped it.

"Lost something?" Mum glanced up.

"Um. No."

"Well, what are you looking for?"

"Um. We're doing staining tomorrow in leatherwork and—ar—I need something to scrub my hands with afterwards."

That should do it. I waited.

Mum went back to her book. "There's an old pumice stone around somewhere. Nicci had it. Or just get the Hand Clean. Ask your father."

"What?" asked Dad.

I told the story again.

"I did have a lump of pumice but the Hand Clean's better. It's under the sink. I'll get it later and put it in your bag for tomorrow."

It isn't easy to eat your breakfast and keep one leg hidden.

"What's up? Do you want to go to the toilet or what?" Mum was watching me pack my schoolbag with one leg hidden behind the other.

"Nope. I'm right," I said. I grabbed another piece of toast and dived for the door. "Bye."

"Well, don't hang on too long," Mum yelled.

I escaped before she launched into her "what-happens-to-old-ladies-if-you-hold-on-too-long" lecture.

"What'd you want a pumice stone for?" asked Beth.

"What's a pumice stone?" put in Sue.

I held out my leg.

97

"Er, yuck," said Beth. "What'd you do that for?"

"Mum said I can't shave my legs till I'm sixteen."

"My mum said that too," said Sue.

I checked her legs—not a hair on them.

"I used one of Dad's razors. Why'd you use a pumice stone? I've never even seen one."

"Didn't your mum notice?"

Sue opened my bag, looking for something to eat. "Nah," she mumbled into its depths. I wasn't surprised. Sue's mum was always in a muddle. I doubt she'd notice if Sue shaved her head. "What've you got the Hand Clean for? Did we have to bring Hand Clean? I haven't got any. Can I use yours? What do we need Hand Clean for? Yuck. It pongs."

"Gotta wash your hands." Beth leered at me. "Just in case. Hey, Sue."

"What?" mumbled Sue, except it sounded like "Woomph" as she munched an apple that had been floating in my bag for ages. She is really gross sometimes.

"Yeah, Sue. Guess who was holding hands with Adrian Simpson?"

I nearly died. Nothing about my life was sacred. Beth had lived her whole life in Bondi and knew everyone. We'd only moved there six months ago, and I still felt like a stranger. Beth also knew everything about everyone, which was all right except when it was you.

"Look at your face," she crowed at me. "It's all red. Who loves Adrian then? Whoa!"

"I dunno," muttered Sue, digging around in my lunch. "That apple was rank. God, Em, don't you ever clean out your bag?"

Beth rolled her eyes. "He wants to meet ya on Saturday."

I swear I stopped breathing. "Oh, yeah, who said?" I asked. Someone showed me once how you turn blue if you hold your breath for too long. I hoped I wasn't blue yet.

"Wouldn't you like to know!" she roared.

I started breathing again. "Go on. Tell me."

I tried to look like I was enjoying this. It was obvious Beth was enjoying it. She pointed her pudgy finger at me and zoomed it into my shoulder. "Who loves Addy-Waddy then?" she crooned.

I swear one day I'll get her. I just don't know how yet. She's weird. Most of the time she's nice, but whenever I do something that's not the same as everyone else she turns rotten. I mean, she really makes me suffer. Like the time I knew all the answers in Biology.

"Listen to her," she'd crowed. "Little Miss Perfect. Been studying for Mr Matthews, have we? Want to be Matthews' pet?"

I never did it again. She called me "Mattie's Pet" for days, and I just had to put up with it. I mean, if Beth didn't talk to me, who would? I hardly knew the other guys, and they all knew each other real well. Everyone I really knew was five hundred kilometres away. Some of these drips had even been to pre-school together. It was always "Remember Andrew Small?" or "Did you hear about Susie's dad?" and all that. I just didn't know them, and if Beth went, then I guess Sue would go too. I mean, they seemed to have been friends for so long. And you know what was really weird? Beth was always right. I did want to be Mr Matthews' pet, and I did love Adrian.

By afternoon my red leg had turned spotty and white. It looked like a rooster's neck when his feathers have been plucked—except that some of my feathers were still there. It was gross. I sat in my usual seat on the bus. I'm up the front. The back seats are for the guys in Year 9, Adrian's year. They barge on and sprawl and tell dirty jokes. I'll bet they're dirty jokes because every now and then the whole bus hears a guffaw and someone jumps up and punches someone else. Someone up there likes to bellow "PISS ORF" at least four times a trip. Then the bus driver looks in his mirror and sends evil messages with his eyes. One day an old lady rang the buzzer and got off where there wasn't even a bus stop. I knew how she felt.

I used to watch the girls up there. They travelled all the way home backwards and they whinnied a lot. It was amazing really, because the boys took no notice of them, except maybe to say "PISS ORF." They never did, though.

Keeping my rooster's neck leg under the seat, I pretended to be really interested in the shops outside. I felt the seat floomp and jammed myself closer to the side of the bus.

"G'day, Emma."

My breath stopped. I read once that air going up your throat makes your voice. It doesn't because I swear I wasn't breathing.

"Hi, Adrian."

My leg was beginning to ache. I wished I'd eaten some Juicy Fruit—it makes your breath smell good. I hoped mine did because I had to breathe soon.

"You going to the beach Saturday?" Adrian seemed to be in a hurry.

"Yeah," I said.

"See ya there." And he was gone. I didn't dare look where, but a guffaw from the back of the bus told me he'd arrived. I hoped my neck wasn't as blue as my face.

Shaving cream is great stuff. I found a can stashed at the back of the bathroom cupboard, left over from the time before Dad grew a beard. It was pretty gross—all rusty round the bottom, and there was white flaky stuff around the top and down one side. I'd had to wait a couple of days until my rooster's rash cleared up. I was also waiting for Mum's yoga class.

"I'll be back about six. You guys can keep out of mischief till then," Mum said, looking straight at me.

"Me and Dad going to the shed," The Mouth said. "Down the shed, Daddy?"

Dad was painting up an old bike with trainer wheels for her.

"Right," he said. "Down the shed. Off we go. Jiggety-jog, jiggety-jog."

Honestly, I don't know how they can behave like that. I mean, The Mouth was going to go just as happily without the jiggety business.

Everything was perfect. The shaving cream, the razor and me. The toilet was just close enough to the bath so I could perch on it to do the job.

The can said to wet the face—well, it wasn't a face, but I wet it anyway. I filled up The Mouth's Tubby Jug and just poured the water on. It ran down my leg, over the floor and into the plughole thing in the middle of the bathroom floor. I listened. Perfect. Not a sound.

Next, the can told me, squeeze the nozzle and apply lather evenly to face and neck. I giggled. I was beginning to enjoy this. I aimed and squeezed hard. Nothing. I tried again. The nozzle was stuck—I think some of the gunk must have got caught or something. I gave it a bash on the bath and out it came. Just everywhere. I actually filled the Tubby Jug, built a little mountain on the toilet seat and caked it down my legs before it stopped. It's amazing how much foam you can fit in one of those cans. I mean, this one wasn't even full. I spread it over my legs. They were beginning to feel itchy but I didn't dare scratch. The razor was brand new. It took a while to work out how to get the cap off the blade. I bet some little grommet had a great time figuring that one out.

I had to bend right down. It wasn't easy. I nearly fell off the toilet seat and all. I decided to start at the front of my leg and I began to drag the razor through the foam.

At that exact moment the door almost burst off its hinges and The Mouth barged in.

"Just goin' to toilet, Emmie," she began, and then peered

closer. "Oh-er, it's bleeting."

It was bleeting all right. There was blood everywhere. I couldn't believe my eyes. It didn't hurt or anything, but there was all this blood. Everywhere. Coming out of my leg.

"Oh-er," bellowed The Mouth. "Get Daddy."

I don't call her The Mouth for nothing. I reckon the whole street knew "Emmie was bleeting" before Dad reached the back door step.

"Shit!" roared Dad. "What're you doing?"

My dad doesn't swear very much, and that did it. I started to bawl. The Mouth started up too. "Emmie bleeting," she yodelled. "Fix Emmieeeeeeeeeee."

Dad was mumbling stuff about "never-any-peace-around-this-place" while he shoved handfuls of toilet roll at me.

"Here, hold this. There. It'll stop the bleeding. And for heaven's sake stop all the noise. Both of you."

He looked at me again and sort of scratched his head. "You'll never learn." He bent down and got the razor. "Look," he said. "Do little strokes. And rinse it. Not great long gashes. You don't reef it out skin and all."

My legs were really itching now. Except for a lump of blue toilet roll they were still caked in white foam. Some of it was a bit pink where it had got mixed with blood. Yuck.

"Well," said Dad, "your mum'll have a fit but you'd better shave the rest. Try not to cut yourself again."

I only cut myself three more times before I finished. The Mouth was speechless.

"Serves you right." Mum had started. "It'll grow back all bristly." The same old story. "For every one hair you've shaved two will grow back. And look at the mess you've made of your leg. Sit right there so I can fix it up."

She flounced off in the direction of the first-aid kit.

Mum's a pretty terrifying Florence Nightingale. I'll never forget the time she fixed my brother's oyster cuts.

"Shut up, Matthew," she'd said. "This doesn't hurt a bit." And she poured this yellow stuff on. I mean, he was roaring and hauling his feet back. I never saw anyone try so hard to suck their feet back into their ankles. She finally had him in a headlock and was going for the fourth cut when she stopped.

"That's funny," she muttered. "Mercurochrome's pink, not yellow." She scratched around in the big Tupperware dish that we use as the first-aid container. "Oh, my God. Guess what I've done. Oh, poor Matthew. Oh, I'm so sorry."

It was really funny. She had actually used iodine instead. Matt had curled up into a ball and he wasn't uncurling for anybody.

"Don't touch me!" he bawled. Florence mumbled something about getting the colours mixed up. "A natural mistake," she'd said. And, "How come nobody told me?"

You can bet I was watching what colour she had when she came back from the bathroom.

Since we've moved nobody calls at our house (well, it's my grandfather's house really) except sometimes people come to see Mum and Dad, so when there was a knock at the door, I didn't even budge. The Mouth raged through with Mum. It must be terrifying to be a visitor at our house, grown-up or not.

"Adrian's here! Adrian's here!" The Mouth roared. Beth would know about this. I'm sure she could hear her.

It really felt funny having a boy there with Mum and Dad. But, you know, they didn't even hassle. I mean, it could have been just a girlfriend.

"Want a cold drink, Adrian?" Mum asked.

"Getting ready for end of year?" Dad said. "How's old Simon going?"

And before you knew it we were all talking. Like, it was that easy.

"Well," said Mum, "I'll put Nicci to bed and you can start

the dishes, Ron."

And then we were alone.

"Came down to tell ya I'll have to see ya at the station Saturday," Adrian said.

I'd expected that was where he'd see me anyway.

"OK," I said. "Who's going?"

"Just the others. Brian and Ros and Jim and Rosemary. Bring some lunch."

We sat there for a while. There didn't seem to be too much to say.

"What'd you do to ya leg? Cut it shaving?"

I should have been embarrassed—stuff like hairs and pimples and dandruff always embarrasses me—but we both sat looking at it.

"Yeah," I laughed. "Yeah." And suddenly there was a lot to say.

Sandra

Max Dann

My early life was troubled. It began turning sour on me the year I turned five, when I was told I was going to have to start school and go outside and mix with other people. I wasn't sure if I wanted to mix with other people.

It was in the same year that I discovered I had inherited a mouthful of unevenly spaced teeth. They were also chalky in consistency, cavity-prone, and discoloured. I realised at an early age that they were going to require constant attention for the better part of my life.

I was born inside a pre-freckled body. I would never tan, only blemish. Not only did I have to give up opening my mouth, but now I had to hide my body in a long-sleeved shirt all year round as well. Things worsened. I developed flat feet, suffered most allergies known to the medical profession, and discovered an inability to communicate socially with any group of people numbering more than two. My hair changed to a shocking shade of red.

As I grew older, say nine or ten, I learned to cope with my various hereditary afflictions in the only way I knew how. I became unhappy. Later, with the discovery that I liked girls, I was forced to face another revelation. They didn't like me back, at least none of the ones I liked, liked me back.

There was very little to look forward to. A life of disappointment. If I didn't die of depression, then I would die of boredom. Every year was the same as the year before. It would start going bad in February, and just go on becoming more miserable from there. Christmas was the worst of all.

Christmas meant Dromana, a bayside resort roughly sixty kilometres south-east of Melbourne. My parents insisted on going down there every summer for a twenty-eight-day card-playing marathon. There was nothing else to do at Dromana. If you didn't play cards, all you had left was knitting and sleeping. The other half of the population, who were all under ten and too young for cards, played marbles and dug up the beach instead. At seventeen, I was a social misfit.

There was nothing to do at Dromana. No nightspots, no wild parties. There weren't even any postcards you could buy to send back to your friends. There was nothing at Dromana worth showing to anybody.

We parked our caravan next to the Fletchers' every year. They were a big-boned, squat, loud couple who happened to have a son, Peter. He was rude, selfish, thoughtless, a bad loser at practically everything, had a warped sense of humour, and didn't like me very much either. Year after miserable year, he was there. The only person my age, and I couldn't talk to him about anything deeper than the price of ice.

Then Sandra arrived. Sandra was dream material. Tall, clear skin, long dark curly hair, good teeth, lively, cool, mystical. She had everything I didn't have. She also had this peculiar way of standing. Her spine arched inwards in the small of her back. I'd always been a sucker for girls with curved spines like that.

Her name was Sandra Hemmings. She was seventeen, unmarried, and was down with her parents from a place called Cohuna, where her father was some kind of farmer.

I became obsessed with Sandra from the first moment I saw her. I'd been wild over girls before, but never quite the way I was over Sandra. The Hemmings had arrived pulling a caravan not quite the size of a suburb. Because of its size it had to be parked up on the hill, overlooking the toilet block. It stood up there looking down over the rest of the park like a town hall. I could see the whole thing from the window over the sink in our caravan.

I spent hours at a time sitting there watching it, catching glimpses of Sandra walking past windows. I didn't always watch it from a sitting down position, though. I spent quite a bit of time watching it on my way to and from the toilets as well. There was a mirror in there and I combed my hair a lot.

"She's going to think you've got some sort of bladder infection," Peter Fletcher said.

Fletcher wasn't interested in girls. He said he had no time for them. He was too busy annoying everybody, I suppose. I was glad of that at least. If Fletcher wasn't interested, that eliminated my only possible competition. But even if he had been interested, I didn't imagine he would have been much competition. Apart from his disagreeable disposition, he wasn't much to look at. Short body, puffy-faced, big thick lips. He had a body like a 44-gallon drum. Standing beside him, I actually didn't look too bad. I did a lot of standing about beside Fletcher for the first couple of days. He was prepared to stand beside anybody who would put up with his snide remarks for a while. I wanted Sandra to know just what was available. Me or Fletcher, that was all there was. We leaned against the toilet block wall mostly. That way she got to see us both whenever she stepped in or out. I felt sure Fletcher was making me look more attractive with each new sighting of the two of us side by side.

Nothing came of it, though. She didn't make any moves anyway. I'd given her more than enough opportunities to come up and start a conversation with me. When she didn't, I realised I wasn't going to be able to rely on good looks alone. I was going to have to talk to her somehow myself.

I spent the next three or four days thinking about what to say. Conversation was not going to be easy. Apart from the fact that we both took showers in the same building, there was nothing I could think of that we had in common.

Then there was another problem. When I did get talking to her and everything, where did I ask her out? There was nowhere to go. A re-run of *Dr Zhivago* was showing at the local picture theatre. But I didn't want to take a girl to see that, it went on all night. Three-and-a-quarter hours. I wanted to try and keep her awake.

A walk along the beach in the moonlight? No, too many things to stand on. If it wasn't a stray spade somebody had left behind, it would be a platoon of soldier crabs. Besides, the entire water's edge was lined with sand castles and man-made moats. You could break an ankle strolling along that beach at night. Perhaps there was some daytime activity? I'd think about it.

In the meantime, Sandra and I spent a day down at the beach together. Not exactly together. I sat a little further along the beach from where she was. But we had it more or less to ourselves. Until Fletcher arrived, anyway. He came and sat next to me. His legs looked like bridge fasts in shorts.

"You said anything to her yet?"

"I keep on being interrupted," I said.

"Interrupted!" he snorted. "You've been sitting down here uninterrupted for four hours. I've been watching you from up at the boat sheds. What are you waiting for, the sands to shift and carry you over there without leaving your towel?"

Fletcher ruined my chances that day.

I had another opportunity to speak to Sandra the following day, though. Conditions were ideal. Fletcher was at least two kilometres away. I was alone, she was alone. We were both on a bus coming back from Rosebud. She looked like she had been up there shopping or something.

I'd been to the dentist. My teeth didn't restrict their falling apart to Melbourne and its environs. I could lose a filling or suffer a gum infection practically anywhere at any time. I'd just had a surface amalgam filling in the upper left. And I'd been given enough injections to deaden the whole left-hand side of my body down to my waist.

It was useless even to try and break the ice. She'd never have understood a word I was saying. I'd had to tell the bus driver where I wanted to go four times before he understood

I was trying to get back to Dromana.

To make matters worse, Sandra recognised me and smiled as she walked on past me along the aisle. I couldn't smile back. Only half of my face was working. The best I could manage was a sort of twisted grimace. I should have just nodded instead.

"She probably thinks you're some sort of sex offender," Fletcher had the thoughtfulness to say when I told him later.

Sandra was driving me mad. She was an itch I couldn't scratch. I had to reach her somehow, there had to be a way. I had become the only person in Dromana who hadn't spoken to her. I'd seen her talking to the park manager, the ice man, the fruiterer and the bread boy. I'd even spotted my own father having a chat with her outside the shower block one morning. Within a week of Sandra's arrival I had plunged into a state of agitated destitution. She was the pearl and I was the oyster. I felt possessed, obsessed, and worn out from constant thinking about her. I couldn't sleep.

Then it happened. Entirely by chance, after I'd long given up any hope of ever talking to her, I did.

I said: "No, I don't think so. Have you tried the Fletchers?"

It was around lunch time, and I was busy peeling skin off my shoulders, sitting in the annexe, when she appeared out of nowhere and stuck her head in. She had caught me completely by surprise. Their dog, Woofer, had run away again. They had brought along a Pekinese dog that belonged to her mother or something. A hostile little animal with a persecution problem, always getting free and terrorising some five-year-old somewhere.

It was the closest I'd ever been to Sandra. I stood up and got so close to her I could smell the soap she'd used to wash herself with in the shower that morning. She looked just as stunning up close as she did from a distance. She asked me if I had seen Woofer. That's when I said, "No, I don't think so. Have you tried the Fletchers?"

She said, "Thanks."

That conversation was the turning point. Now that we had broken the speech barrier, it would be just a matter of timing.

The solution came to me later that evening. I was sitting in the annexe swatting mosquitoes. Fletcher was there, of course. He had come over to pick his toenails in front of me with his fish knife. He was exaggerating about some fish somebody was supposed to have caught off the pier that afternoon. By his description of its size they would have needed nothing less than a trawler and a crane to pull it out of the water, and . . . then it came to me!

Fish. Fish! Of course, fish would be perfect! That was it. I'd call on the Hemmings with some fish, and say I'd been out all night fishing and had caught too many. Would they like some? They would say yes, invite me over to lunch. I'd act surprised, humble, and would accept graciously. It was brilliant! There were some fish in the icebox, my mother had bought them the day before. They would still be fresh enough. I'd take them over first thing in the morning.

I still couldn't sleep. Now I was too happy. I lay awake on my stretcher for close on four hours, imagining, planning, picturing myself sitting at the same table as Sandra. What would the Hemmings like to talk about, I wondered. It didn't matter: whatever it was, I'd join in.

Finally I did get to sleep. I know, because I woke up later. Much later. It was 10.30. I didn't rush over to the Hemmings' caravan straight away. I wanted to arrive just before lunch time. I used my free time to prepare myself. I never looked terrific in the middle of the day, but I wanted to do my best.

I shaved, trimmed my nails, cleaned my nails, combed my hair for almost twenty minutes, brushed my teeth, ironed a shirt, cleaned my shoes. I stepped out of our annexe looking like a drink waiter. Getting the fish had been no problem. My parents had left a note saying they had gone shopping. I took all six fish out and flopped them into a big plastic bowl.

It was hot. Awnings had been pulled down, curtains had been drawn, and the park was almost empty of all life. Most of the people there were down on the beach already. The Hemmings weren't, though.

I passed the Fletchers' van, went on around the toilet block, and began climbing the small incline. My feet felt heavy, weighted. My body suddenly felt sluggish, as if I hadn't been asleep at all. I was overdressed. I should have come more casual. The Hemmings wouldn't have minded.

I reached the top of the hill. I was exhausted. I put the plastic bowl down on the grass, then sat down too. Beside me there was a block of ice melting into a thin pool of water. I watched it go on shrinking for a while.

That was all that was left of the Hemmings. A small block of discarded ice and some tyre tread marks. They had pulled out.

I don't know how long I went on sitting there. But I was still sitting there when Fletcher came over. He was wearing a pair of towelling shorts and a matching shirt. He looked like a gigantic ten-year-old.

"The Hemmings have gone. They left early this morning."

"I know that! Do you think I'm stupid or something?" I snapped.

"About seven," he went on. "I helped the old man pull down the annexe. They wanted to stay longer, but one of their bulls had some sort of turn and started chasing the cows around or something. They enjoyed themselves, though, said they'd probably come back again next year." He paused, and peered into the bowl as if he had just that moment noticed it. "Been fishing?"

I didn't answer. I wasn't listening. Next year, they were coming back next year then! I'd have a car next year! And money, too, I'd be starting work soon. I'd have that much more experience then as well. All the ground work had been laid out. There was still hope.

D.G. Loves A.R. True!

Dianne Bates

When we were in first year at high school my friend Doris Gulgong had a crush on a teacher. His name was Alex Rostrum, but everyone called him Rooster. Nobody except Doris liked Rooster. He taught French and could never understand why we hadn't mastered the subject under his expert guidance.

"It's not 'silver plate'," he'd scream, doing a war-dance of frustration. "It's *s'il vous plaît*. Repeat after me, *s'il vous plaît*."

"Silver plate," we'd chorus back at him.

None of the teachers liked our class very much. Perhaps it had something to do with the time Marshall Fielding was secretly smoking in class and his desk caught fire. Or when Spike Harrison put rotten egg gas in the staff room for a joke. Or when Judith Webber started a rumour that Mr Watson, the Maths teacher, was having an affair with the Deputy Principal, Ms Baldwin. Mrs Watson caused a scene in the playground when she found out.

So our French lessons with Rooster continued, and with each lesson he grew more and more sarcastic. For some insane reason Doris grew more and more enamoured.

"I just love the way he says, 'It's not "mercy buttercups", you morons, it's *merci beaucoup*'," Doris mooned. "His eyes flash like neon lights when he's mad . . . He's so spunky!"

"Spunky!" I replied, reeling under her interpretation of the word. "Why, he must be fifty if he's a day! And besides, if he's so spunky, how come he hasn't got a girlfriend?"

"He's just shy," Doris said by way of excuse. "Notice how

he blushes every time one of us girls winks at him?" This was true. Once we'd discovered that Rooster was prone to blushing, we flirted madly with him at every opportunity just for the pleasure of watching his face ripen to a cherry red.

"I don't know why you can't see his natural charm and sex appeal," Doris went on.

Doris had a reputation for insanity, so I forgave her. It's hard to be normal when you're the daughter of the head of the Languages Department. Besides, I liked her. And I felt sorry for her, too: she was asthmatic and missed a lot of school.

The rest of us, though, were getting pretty sick of Rooster's sarcasm as well as his ridiculous French translations, so, egged on by Marshall Fielding and his offsider Spike, we set out to make Rooster's life as miserable as he made ours. Someone found out—quite by accident—that Rooster was allergic to flowers, so bunches of flowers started appearing on the teacher's desk every time we had French lessons.

The first time they appeared, Rooster sniffed the air suspiciously as soon as he walked into the room. Then he started sniffling and his eyes watered. He pulled the flowers out of the vase, went out on to the balcony, and threw them as far as he could. Inside the classroom we all moaned. But we hadn't counted on Alice McInerny. Everyone—guys especially—had a soft spot for Alice with her flawless skin and baby blue eyes. Alice wanted to be an actress when she left school, and this incident was great practice for her budding career. She pretended to be really upset about Rooster tossing out the flowers, and she did it so well that after a while I wondered if she wasn't genuine.

"I grew them myself, just so I could give them to you, sir," she said in a tearful voice, ". . . and you threw them out."

The class held its breath. Rooster reddened. Alice sniffed. And Doris grunted with disgust.

"I'm sorry," Rooster said gruffly. "I didn't realise."

Alice rewarded him with a Nobel Prize of a smile and we

watched as a wave of crimson washed over his face. Alice's talent was astounding!

"Bitch," Doris muttered beside me.

So we continued to bring flowers to school every day we had French. And each time Rooster would smile kindly at Alice and say, "I'm sorry, but I get hay fever. I'll just leave them up here on the cupboard near the window away from the desk, where I can see them." And Alice would smile coyly in her best Hollywood style.

One day Rooster hit on the bright idea of using conversational French in class.

"What's that?" Alice asked.

"What do you think it is?" he replied.

"I dunno. Is it a French word?"

Rooster thumped his forehead. "And they teach you English!" he moaned. "I want the class to talk in French all through the lesson, starting from now."

"Sir, that's not fair!" Judith Webber yelled. Rooster roared back at her in French (I think he told her to shut up). The thunder in his voice silenced us.

Only a few goody-goodies in the class—Kate Curran, Sean Gilchrist, Muscles Mayné, Cheryl Mannix and love-struck Doris—showed any enthusiasm. The rest of us slumped down in our desks, hoping not to be chosen. After a while Marshall and Spike and some of the other kids started flicking paper pellets around the classroom when Rooster wasn't looking. The girls were passing notes. One landed on my desk. It read: *I found out Mrs Green's first name. It's Delvene.* (Mrs Green was our music teacher.)

I looked across at Doris, trying to catch her attention so I could chuck the note to her. But Doris didn't seem interested. Her face was as white as a sheet, and she was gasping for breath. I could tell she was having an asthma attack. I put my hand up.

"Sir, Doris is sick," I said.

Doris glared at me. She hated missing Rooster's class: she would sit through hell and high water—asthma, even—to be in the same room, breathing the same air as her beloved Mr Rostrum.

"I think you'd better go to Sick Bay, Doris," Rooster said.

"You spoke in English!" Judith roared accusingly at him.

This time he ignored her. He helped Doris to her feet. I thought Doris was going to faint—not from asthma, but because her darling had held her arm. I knew she would never wash that arm again.

"Whoo, hoo, sir's in love with Gulgong!" whistled Spike.

"Are you all right?" Rooster asked Doris. She nodded. You could see she was too choked up with asthma (and love) to talk.

"Off you go then," Rooster said to her.

Then he walked to the front of the room. "*Ouvrez les livres,*" he commanded.

We looked at one another, puzzled, then watched Muscles, Cheryl and a few others open their books. I waved at Doris as she walked out of the room. She ignored me.

The translation exercise that Rooster set was difficult. I laboured over it, and was looking up at the ceiling for inspiration, trying to think of the French word for "bananas", when Rooster picked up a piece of paper near my foot. I realised it was the note about Mrs Green that I'd been trying to pass on to Doris.

Rooster looked at me. "Small things amuse small minds," he said.

"I never wrote it!" I protested.

"Get on with your work," he growled.

I lowered my head again to the trials of foreign words. Before I put pen to paper, however, Alice's flowers worked their effect; Rooster let fly a series of sneezes that sounded like a backfiring Kawasaki. Everyone laughed.

"Ged od wid your work!" he roared.

Moments later the quiet of the room was shattered by Rooster demanding, "Who did this?"

I looked up. He was standing by the wastepaper bin, waving another scrap of paper at the class.

"Did you write this, Deborah Mitchell?"

"What is it?" I asked.

Rooster came up and shoved it under my nose.

(heart with arrow through it containing "D. G. loves A. R." and the word "TRUE" written beside it)

"This!" His face was red and blotchy. I had never seen him so mad.

I recognised the writing immediately. Doris must have thrown the paper out on her way to Sick Bay, and Rooster had spied it when he went to throw the note about Mrs Green in the bin.

"I never wrote it," I protested again.

"Who did?"

"I don't know."

"What is it, Debbie?" Judith Webber strained to read it from the back of the room.

Rooster fixed her with one of his famous "I've-spotted-the-trouble-maker" looks, threw back his head and crowed, "Aha!" Then his expression changed. "I might have guessed you would have something to do with this, Miss Webber," he sneered.

Judith stood up, her hands on her hips. "I don't know what you're talking about," she said.

"I will not have rumours about *me* circulating around this school!" Rooster declared.

By now the rest of the class were as curious as cats. "What's going on?" they asked.

Again Judith and I declared our innocence.

Nobody would own up to having written what Rooster declared was "a vile piece of slander".

"You will all be kept in during lunch hour," he told the class. "And you will be kept in every day until the person responsible owns up. I've had enough of this class and its idiotic little games."

Of course nobody was prepared to admit guilt. And Doris was still in Sick Bay. By the time Rooster released us from detention, ten minutes before the end of the lunch period, everyone was fuming. Most of them blamed Judith and me for the note.

"One of youse had better tell pretty soon, or there'll be trouble," Marshall threatened.

After school I went around to Doris's place to tell her the grim news. When she met me at the door, I could tell straight away that she knew.

"My father," she said. "He heard Mr Rostrum talking about it in the staff room. Mr Rostrum thinks the note was about him and Mrs Green."

"But Mrs Green is married. I don't get it," I said.

"You remember the rumour Judith put around about Mr Watson and Ms Baldwin?"

I nodded.

"Well, Mr Rostrum thought you or Judith were starting another rumour. About him and Mrs Green. Mrs *Delvene* Green . . . D.G."

"Oh no! He thinks D.G. is Delvene Green, and really it's you." I sat down. "What are you going to do?"

Doris was white. "I think I'd better go and tell him the truth before it goes any further," she said.

Poor Doris. She never really recovered from the experience of owning up. Rooster didn't help either; for the rest of the year he avoided Doris like she had some terrible tropical disease. Her father was furious with her, and she had the worst asthma attack of her life.

The best thing to come of it, though, was that quite suddenly Doris fell out of love with Rooster. Her top marks in French plummeted to failures.

After that, Doris started concentrating on numbers. She had fallen for the new Maths teacher, Mr Johnson. Everyone called him "Legs Eleven", and I must admit he was cute! She had a bit of opposition, though. Alice and Judith and some of the other girls in the class tried fluttering their eyelashes at him and hinting that they were available. By the end of the term Mr Johnson quit to go and teach in an all boys' school. He told Doris's father it was a lot safer there than staying on with all us Year 7 girls chasing after him!

Down the Mall

Sally Farrell Odgers

Lalla Astall is my friend. I'd better make that clear straight away! Lalla Astall is my friend. Lalla Astall is also a bit of a bitch.

Maybe that doesn't sound like a very nice thing to say about a friend, but it happens to be true. She isn't one of those people who's all sweet to your face and then stabs you in the back, and then chucks a mental if you do the same thing back. I mean, if she gets mad she says all those poisonous things right to your face, and she's just the same with everyone.

Lalla doesn't have to try hard to get what she wants. Things just naturally go her way. Look. Lalla and I get the same marks for English, more or less, but if Lalla submits a story to the school magazine and I submit a story to the school magazine, and there's only room to print one of them, Lalla's is the one that gets chosen. If I want to go anywhere after dinner, I really get the inquisition from my parents. But Lalla just tells *her* mum she's going out, and she goes. And if there are only two seats left on the bus, and one's beside Spotty Morris and the other's beside Dreamy Kennedy (who's in Year 10), guess who winds up sitting next to Spotty Morris? Lalla Astall? Guess again. Kelly Potter? Who else? But I don't blame *her* .

Lalla and I go down the Mall sometimes for Friday night shopping. Amanda and Sophie and Joanne mostly go too, and sometimes Elizabeth Kennedy, who isn't really one of our bunch. We try on shoes and things, and check out the testers in Fitzies. Mum always goes off at me when I get home, because she can smell me all the way up the garden path. I know that can't be true, though, because it's a proven fact that your senses get duller as you get older, and Mum was forty last month. Anyway, we've never tried more than four different perfumes at any one time, because Lalla says that'd be tacky. Sometimes we don't get past two: one on each wrist, where your pulse points are. Once Lalla and I went to get her eyelashes tinted, because we're not allowed to wear mascara at school, and Lalla's blonde and her eyelashes are sort of sandy.

We always have a coffee at the tables outside Nutmegs Café and watch the people who come to the Mall. Amanda and Joanne and Sophie have a sort of game where they give points out of twenty to the guys. It's a pity they never score any higher than seven. On the whole, they're a pretty gross looking lot.

"Why is it," says Amanda, at least every second Friday, "that we never see any decent ones? They're all weedy and spotty or red and beefy. Er-yuck, I mean, fancy being kissed by one of those . . ."

"Probably all the good ones have got something better to do than hang round down the Mall," says Lalla.

"What d'you mean?" Amanda's usually spoiling for a fight. "*We're* hanging round down the Mall."

"We are, aren't we?" says Lalla, and gets up. "Come on, Kel. Let's go." So we go. But sometimes, if we're on our own, Lalla can be really funny. She says things about the guys that really break me up. I suppose it really isn't very nice of her, but it's fun. Well, it used to be, but things have started to change since the beginning of the summer holidays.

The Friday school broke up, we were heading down the Mall to finish our Christmas shopping. While we were sorting through the bargain trays, Joanne poked me in the ribs. "Hey, don't look now," she said, out of the side of her mouth like a spy. So of course we all looked. There was Elizabeth Kennedy, sitting outside Nutmegs with a boy. He was one of the skinny, spotty ones that always smell of KleraSkin, but when she saw us looking she beckoned us over and introduced him like he was Mel Gibson at least. He didn't say much, but she did enough talking for both of them. Then she sort of flipped her hand at us, and he did the same, and we went on our way.

"What'd you think?" I said to Lalla, while the others were all giggling and carrying on.

"I think it's a pity about his nose," said Lalla quite loudly. the others all looked at her. Everyone always looks at Lalla when she speaks up.

"What about it?" said Amanda. "What was wrong with it?"

"Nothing really," said Lalla. "I mean, he'd be a real find for a jazz band if they needed a spare trombone."

"Do you reckon it gets in the way when he kisses her?" Joanne wanted to know.

Amanda let out a squawk. "Kisses her? Kisses Elizabeth? She'd never let him!"

We all laughed at that, because, honestly, Elizabeth's the sort of girl who even brings her toothbrush to school, and she never reads anything hotter than *Family Circle*.

When Christmas and New Year were over, things seemed a bit flat, so I was pleased when Amanda rang up to ask if I wanted to go down the Mall in the afternoon. "Joanne's coming," she said, "but I couldn't get Sophie."

"What about Lalla?" I said.

"Haven't asked her," said Amanda. So I called around at Lalla's place on the way. Lalla was on her own, reading a magazine, and she said she'd come.

"Going to leave a note for your mum?" I said.

"What for?" said Lalla, combing her hair.

"Oh—I just thought you might," I said.

Lalla only shrugged, so I followed her out without saying anything else.

There were some people busking in the Mall. I thought they

were good until Lalla pointed out that the girl looked like something left over from the 1960s. After that, all I could see was her floppy hair and the sort of limp cotton thing she was wearing. She looked really weird.

"Where's Sophie?" said Joanne while Lalla was trying on some shoes.

"Gone to her Gran's, I s'pose," said Amanda. "She mostly does."

"Daggy," said Joanne, pulling a face. "I've got to go to the shack with my aunt later this month."

"What on earth for?" said Amanda.

"Babysitting my little cousins," said Joanne. "At least it's not my Gran's . . . that'd be . . ." Joanne's voice trailed off, because Amanda had stopped listening.

"Hey, will ya look at that!" Amanda said in a funny sort of voice. We looked, of course, and there were Sophie and this boy walking along like they were glued together. Since Sophie's pretty tall and this boy was a bit of a weed, the effect was pretty peculiar, but still . . .

"Get them!" said Amanda, loudly. Sophie never let on she'd heard—well, she mightn't have. She just twined herself further round this boy's neck. It's a wonder they could walk at all. Joanne and I stared. Then Lalla showed up. She'd finished with the shoes and she was a bit pissed off with me because I hadn't gone with her to try them on.

"Look over there," I said.

Lalla looked at Sophie. It was a funny sort of look, as if she was trying to work something out. Well, you couldn't really blame her. "Poor Sophie," she said.

"What d'you mean, *poor*?" Joanne wanted to know.

"No discrimination," said Lalla. "Must be desperate, otherwise she'd throw that one back until it'd grown a bit."

We all giggled. I felt a bit mean, but Sophie's not that much of a friend, not like Lalla. Besides, she couldn't hear us. That's why I was a bit surprised when she rang me up a couple of days later. Sophie did, I mean. "Can I come over?" she said.

I said she could. I wanted to hear all about it.

"Well?" I said, as soon as she sat down on the porch.

"Well what?" said Sophie, looking at her fingernails.

"*Tell* me," I said.

"Tell you what?" said Sophie, but she couldn't keep a straight face.

"About that boy you were with the other day, of course! What's his name? Where did you meet him?"

It turned out that his name was Rod Collins and he was a friend of Sophie's brother Sam. He and Sam had been fixing Sam's motor bike up at Sophie's place, and when they'd finished with that, they were going to start doing Rod's.

"Not that they're making much progress!" said Sophie, and giggled. It might have been hard to get her talking, but soon she was rattling on like a DJ. It was Rod Collins says this, and Rod Collins thinks that, and Rod Collins does the other. I wondered if he'd done Sophie yet, but she didn't say, and there are some things you don't ask even your friends . . . especially not your friends, because sometimes they tell you and then later on wish they hadn't. But they always know that *you* know, and pretty soon they start to hate you for knowing.

"Rod Collins knows all about cars already," said Sophie. "He's going to be an apprentice at Mudge's Garage in March. His brother works there already but Rod Collins says that hasn't got anything to do with how he got on. He knows more than his brother already."

I noticed she always called him "Rod Collins", like that, as if it was one word. I wondered why she didn't just call him "Rod" or "my boyfriend", or something like that.

She came up again a couple of days later. I got pretty sick of hearing about Rod Collins, and I was wishing she'd go home when Lalla arrived. Sophie just nodded at her, which I thought was a bit rude, and went on telling me how Rod

Collins had found out what was wrong with her brother Sam's bike after two qualified mechanics had given it up. "It only needed a new sprocket, Rod Collins says, and they ought to have known all along. He knew straight away as soon as he looked at it."

Lalla listened for a while, then she said, "Rod Collins? Now, where have I heard that name before?" She snapped her fingers a few times, the way you do when you're trying to remember something. "Oh yes, isn't he that kid we saw you with down the Mall?"

Sophie stared, then nodded. "That's right, but he's not a kid. He was seventeen last week."

"Oh!" said Lalla. "I didn't think he was that old. I don't suppose he'll ever grow any more, then."

Sophie turned red and didn't say much more about Rod Collins. She hardly mentioned him the next time she came up to my place, and the time after that she didn't say anything at all.

"What's happened to Rod Collins?" I said.

She shrugged and then looked at herself in my mirror, really close, like she was looking for open pores. "Dunno," she said, when I asked her again. "Haven't seen him lately. Not that I care. He's a bit immature, don't you think?"

"I thought you were going to the pictures Wednesday night."

"So did I," said Sophie, "but he never showed."

"P'raps he was sick," I said.

She shrugged again. "No, because I went round to his place on Thursday and he was working on his bike."

"What did you say?" I asked, thinking that if it had been me, I'd have shrivelled up.

"I said what had happened," said Sophie, "and he said he'd been busy. I said, well, the film was going to be on Saturday too, but he just went on mucking about with the bike."

"What'd you do?" I said.

"I had better things to do than hang around watching, so I went home. Well, I've got my pride, haven't I?" She sniffed, and I said why didn't she come down the Mall on Friday, and she said she might as well. Before she came I told the others she'd broken up with Rod Collins, so they didn't say anything to her about it.

We did all the usual things, but I kept seeing all these other girls with their boyfriends. I'd never taken much notice before, but now that Sophie had had a boyfriend—well, a sort of one—that brought it all closer. I started wondering what they all did together. I mean, I know they wandered about with their arms round one another, and looked in shop windows down the Mall, but they didn't seem to do much talking.

"Oh . . . *talking*," said Amanda. "Who wants to talk?", and Joanne and even Sophie giggled.

Joanne went away babysitting pretty soon after, and when she came back she had a great tan and a new camera. When we went down the Mall that week, she said she had to go into Quik Pix to collect her photos. We all went in with her.

"These the right ones?" asked the woman behind the counter, and she opened the folder the way they do so you can make sure you've got your photos and not somebody else's by mistake. Joanne had a quick look at the top one and nodded and went to take the folder, but Amanda went "Heeey!", like that, and got it first. Joanne grabbed for it, but we could see she didn't really mind if we looked, so when she got Amanda by the arm Amanda threw the folder to me. I missed, and the photos fanned out in the air and pattered on to the floor. The woman behind the counter had a "Well, really!" look on her face, but we were feeling a bit manic by then so we just shovelled up the photos and passed them round. Lalla hung back, which wasn't like her, and went over to look through a stack of giant posters over by the counter.

Most of the pictures had been taken at the beach. There

were a few of Joanne's little cousins, but the ones we were interested in were of Joanne standing with her arm round a guy and one of the same guy by himself with a stubby in his hand.

"Heeey! Where did you find him?" said Amanda.

Joanne went a blotchy red under her tan. "Oh, him?" she said, and I could see she was trying to pretend it wasn't that important. "I met him down at the beach. He's on holiday from Uni."

"Show us!" said Sophie, sticking out her hand. She had another new nailpolish on. She's a lot taller than I am, but I sort of peered past her shoulder to get a look at Joanne's boy. Well—young man, really. He looked about twenty. He had a tan and he was wearing the sort of bathers that are hardly there; I mean, where can you look?

"Heeey!" said Amanda again. It was starting to get to me. Sophie looked a bit sick too . . . I suppose she was thinking about Rod Collins. When Amanda had finished drooling, she went to give the pictures back to Joanne.

"Lalla hasn't had a look yet," I said. "Hey, Lal! Come here!"

Lalla propped the posters back against the counter and came over. I passed her the photo that showed the guy on his own. She took it by the edges, very carefully, like she was trying to keep from getting thumbprints on it, only with her it was more like she was trying to keep her hands clean than the photo. She looked at it for about a minute with this funny little smile, and after a bit even Amanda stopped raving on.

"Well?" said Amanda.

Lalla handed the photo back to Joanne, then wiped her hands down the legs of her acid-wash jeans.

"Quite something, isn't he?" said Sophie, smiling determinedly.

"If you like that sort of thing," said Lalla, and went back to finish looking through the posters.

"Lalla—" I said, but she wasn't listening.

Joanne went blotchy red again, but this time she didn't look pleased, and Amanda stopped grinning. "What's with *her*?" she asked, waving her thumb over to where Lalla was.

"She's jealous! Lalla's jealous!" said Sophie, like she'd just made the discovery of the century.

"Of course she isn't," I said. Well, I had to stick up for Lalla, didn't I?

"Bet she is," said Sophie.

"Nah, she couldn't be," said Amanda, shaking her head. "She's just trying to act cool. C'mon, Joanne, let's go and check out the record bar.

Joanne forced her photos into a curved shape so she could shove them into her pocket, then she and Amanda went out.

"Coming, Kel?" asked Sophie.

I looked back at Lalla. "Hey, Lalla, we're going to the record bar. Want to come?" Lalla didn't want to, so I told Sophie I'd see her later. After all, Lalla's my friend. Sophie went after the others and Lalla came away from the posters and we went down the Mall. Lalla was really funny about Joanne's guy. She said he looked like an advert for toothpaste or some sort of drink.

"Stubbies?" I said, and Lalla laughed.

"No, nothing like *that*," she said. "Some new sort of fake wine, I should think. You know . . . 'You Don't Have to Drink to be a Man!'." She spoke in this really deep sort of voice and puffed her chest out like one of those body-builders on telly. Lalla can be really funny when she wants to be.

That happened a couple of weeks ago. Lalla and I went down the Mall the next weekend, but the others all went to the pictures instead. They didn't ask us. I don't care, and Lalla says they're all a bit immature anyway. I don't know about that, but I haven't had too much time to work it out, because the other day Dad got flu so I had to take his dog for a walk. Swaggo's a crazy dog, and he started a fight with another dog this guy was walking in the other direction. It could have been awful, but Darren (the guy) just laughed it off. I ran into him again yesterday, and today he was waiting for me when Swaggo hauled me out our gate.

Tomorrow's Friday, and Darren's asked me if I want to go out somewhere with him. He made a sort of joke about it, saying he promised he wouldn't take his dog if I promised I wouldn't bring mine. I told him Swaggo was Dad's dog, and he said, "Thank goodness for that," but he was smiling when he said it. I really like him.

I've just rung Lalla to say I won't be going down the Mall with her tomorrow. She really sounded pissed off when I told her, and wanted to know why I couldn't go, but I pretended Mum was calling me and hung up.

I feel a bit sorry for Lalla, really. I mean, fancy not liking anyone! All the same, I'm glad I didn't tell her.

Lalla's my friend, but I don't want her to know about Darren yet.

Jonathon's Story

Nette Hilton

Jonathon was frozen. This was, without a doubt, the dumbest idea he'd ever been sucked into.

Sleep on the beach. Oh, yeah. Great idea.

They'd all rushed home and grabbed sausages, sleeping bags, mozzie spray (not necessary in winter) and whatever dirty books they could find.

"It'll be hidjus!" Jacko had said.

Oh, yeah!

Clint had even hinted that it would be a bit cold, but did they listen? No way, José. Now look at them.

Jonathon sat thinking miserably of his nice warm dry bed. He glanced at Clint. He looked like he might have been thinking the same thing. Only Jacko seemed oblivious to the cold drizzle that seeped into every crease in the tent. Maybe it would have helped if they'd used tent poles instead of the metre-long stick Clint had assured them would fit.

Jacko closed the February 1986 copy of *Playboy* and looked at them. "You know what I reckon?" he mused.

"What this time?"

"I reckon it'd be easier in summer."

"What?"

"Sex."

Jonathon glanced over at him. He was pretty sure the sum total of Jacko's sexual experience was the day they'd watched Clint's dog, Ralph, mate with the bull terrier bitch down the road. That, and the day they'd found the copy of *Sexual Happiness* in the book shop in town.

"How'd you figure that?" Jonathon moved around to warm his other side.

"Stands to reason, doesn't it?" Jacko went on plugging up a leak with the mozzie spray can.

"What reason?"

"Well, in summer they only wear bikinis."

"So?"

"So how're you gonna get all their clothes off in winter?"

Silence. Clint didn't know the answer. Neither did Jonathon. "You could ask 'em," he ventured.

"Oh yeah. Yeah. You gotta keep kissin' 'em or they go cold. How're you gonna ask 'em to get their gear off, keep kissin' 'em, and get your own off as well? Have a look!" And Jacko stuck a foot out from under the blankets. "I got on footy socks and gym boots. Go on. How're you gonna do it?"

Jonathon had to admit he really didn't have an answer. "Maybe you could leave 'em on."

"What?"

"Your boots."

"Can't get jeans off over your boots."

Clint was obviously puzzled too. He actually sat up. "You know, you could sort of slide 'em down. Half way."

"Oh yeah," the Master replied. "And what about your jumper, and her jumper and tights. Forget it. Can't be done. Ya gotta get their clothes off. And keep kissin' 'em."

Clint crawled further back into the tent. "You know what I reckon?"

"What?" asked Jacko.

"You're a sandwich short of a picnic basket."

And then it really started to rain.

It kept on raining. Right through Sunday and Monday. Real pick-handle stuff. Jonathon sat in the classroom and watched as it sleeted across the playing fields, turning this afternoon's sports area into a swamp. The whole room smelled like mouldy sweatshirts, wet hair and damp bodies. He tried again to listen to Guffy.

". . . and so it becomes obvious why these two elements combined . . ." Poor old Guffy. Jonathon doubted that anyone was listening. He shifted his gaze across the room. His head still ached from the cold he'd caught camping out on the beach. He grinned, though, when he caught sight of The Guff's boots. Good, solid, laced-up work boots—no nonsense stuff, those. There was no way you'd roll your jeans off over them. Jacko was probably right, though. He glanced around the classroom. Strewth, there were enough skivvies, jumpers, tights, tracksuit pants, blouses and gloves to equip an army intent on a six-month march across Alaska. Jonathon sighed and eased himself up. It was then he noticed Jenny Sommerville. She was watching him. Jonathon straightened up a little more and knocked the test-tube rack to the floor.

"Aaah. Welcome back, Jones," quipped The Guff. "Feeling rested, are we?"

Jonathon could feel Jenny's eyes on him. He waited till The Guff had had enough, and then looked back at her.

"*Boring*," she mouthed, and grinned. Jonathon grinned back. He liked Jenny, and just lately he seemed to be noticing her more. They'd shared a canoe during summer sport. Jonathon had hoped she'd continue to be his partner, but Mrs Elliott had lumped him with Jacko. Hopeless! He could still remember how her costume kept sliding up over her bum when she leaned forward to paddle. And how it clung to her when they'd tipped over. He looked at her again. Underneath the jumper, skivvy, uniform and whatever else she'd packed on, it was all still there. Jonathon groaned.

"Yes, Jones? What now?" The Guff turned around.

"Nothing, sir."

"You unwell?"

"Er, no sir. Um, headache. Slight headache. Sir."

Jacko snorted, and somewhere behind him somebody sniggered.

"Do you need to go to sick bay?"

"No sir." The last thing Jonathon wanted at this moment was to stand up. Part of him already was.

"No, sir, I'm fine now. Thank you."

"Sprung," sneered Jacko from behind. "Serves ya right."

But Jonathon kept his eyes on Guffy and the confusion he'd written all over the board. At least Guff was good for something.

"Thank God!" Jenny caught up with him. "That was *so boring*. You OK?"

"Yeah," Jonathon said. "Yeah, I'm fine. So, um, you been doing any canoeing?" Great stuff, Jonno. In mid-winter you're asking her if she's been canoeing.

But she didn't seem to notice. "Nah. Too cold."

They walked a little way in silence. Jonathon tried to look preoccupied with the walls.

"You seen *The Gargantuan*?" Jenny asked.

"Nah. Any good?"

"Yeah. Hot. Should come round and watch it."

Jonathon slowed down. "You seen *Eternal*?"

Jenny grinned. "Yeah. That was real creepy. Specially when the arm floated up through the drain. Yuck!" She paused. "So, um, do you wanna come round? Have to be Saturday. Week nights are out in my house." She pulled a face.

"S'pose," Jonathon said. "Will I bring somethin' to eat?"

"She's cool. Hey, Cath! Wait up! Jonno, gotta go. See ya Saturday. After dinner. I'll check ya later."

She grinned again and galloped off after Cathy. Jonathon watched her. *Unreal*.

"See you sooooooooon," Jacko's voice crooned.

"Get stuffed."

"I won't," Jacko smirked, "but you might."

Before Jonathon could catch him, he'd shoved his bag on to Clint, tripped over three Year 7s, and was gone.

Jonathon sat on the edge of the bath. What if Jacko was right? What if that was what she wanted him for? Didn't seem likely. But what if it was? Dumb choice. Jonathon looked at his reflection. Sloppy joe, shirt, jeans, footy socks and Adidas. He tried sliding down his jeans. They jammed around his footy socks. He looked again. Ridiculous. He couldn't even get his own gear off, let alone anything else. He shuffled closer to the mirror to explore a pimple on his neck. But if she wanted to do it she'd take her own clothes off. Wouldn't she? Jonathon paused. Nope. Definitely didn't seem likely. He thought back to the last R-rated movie he'd watched. The guy in that was definitely dressed. So was the woman. They'd sort of fused together and melted to the floor. Next scene—naked in bed. Jonathon went back to his pimple. Somewhere between the melting and the bed they'd got their gear off. Lying down. Seemed bloody unlikely. Jonathon tried melting.

"Jonathon?" Mrs Jones looked in. "What are you doing? Why are you kneeling down there? You OK?"

"Yeah, Mum. Fine. Just, um, trying a new, um, basketball move."

"Well, could you do it somewhere else? I want to get in here."

"Yeah, right. Just two minutes, OK, Mum?"

Jonathon waited till she'd gone, breathed a sigh of relief, and pulled up his jeans.

"Just doin' some homework, Mum. OK?"

"Sure." Mrs Jones turned around. "You feeling all right?"

"Fine. Just fine." Jonathon closed the door. Now, all he had to do was melt down again and get his clothes off. He melted. No worries. He lay there gazing at the ceiling.

"Keep kissin'," Jacko had said. Jonathon puckered. Didn't work. What he really needed was something to hold on to. That guy in the R-rated movie obviously did. Jonathon looked around the bedroom. Nothing. Except—he almost laughed—except good old Auntie Vi. There she was: Mrs Jones's answer to his nightmares and things that went bump in the night when he was little.

Auntie Vi was a life-sized calico doll. She wore an old dress and shawl from Vinnie's, and had real glasses and corduroy boots laced up with ribbons. Her woollen hair was tied up in a bun. Perfect. She'd taken care of nightmares and night monsters, and now she was going to help Jonathon fulfil a dream.

Jonathon hauled her out of the corner and clutched her to him. R-rated movies were never like this. He melted to the floor with his face firmly glued to Auntie Vi's. Her knees tended to bend the wrong way, but that didn't matter. He kept melting, and not for an instant did he take his mouth from Auntie Vi's dusty felt lips. He lay down, heaved the buckle open on his belt, and squirmed and twisted until he got his jeans down to his footy socks. He buried his face in Auntie Vi's shawl and pulled her dress zipper down. So far, so good. He slid his leg over Vi's to get a good grip on the dress, then shifted his face back to Vi's and dragged her dress over her calico shoulder.

"Jonathon?" His father was bending over him.

Jonathon froze.

"Jonathon?" Mr Jones stepped over him and sat on the edge of the bed. "What are you doing to Auntie Vi?"

"Er, wrestling, Dad. Tryin' some new holds."

"Oh, yeah. You gonna kiss her to death?"

"Nope. Um, it, um, helps to keep my head immobilised."

"Right. I can buy that." Mr Jones leaned forward. "The jeans around the knees. This is a handicap?"

"Yes, sir. That's it. A handicap."

"Right. Well, when you finish dressing Auntie Vi—her dress is all undone there and you dragged her shoulder out—when you finish, your mum said to tell you dinner's ready."

"I'll be right there." Jonathon tried to scramble up.

"I'm sure you will." Mr Jones climbed back over him. "Oh, and Jonathon."

"Yes?"

"If Auntie Vi should suddenly give birth, I'll hold you responsible."

The rest of the week crawled by. Auntie Vi now lived in the lounge-room and serenely watched TV from a rocking chair. Jonathon's mum watched him a lot and kept asking if he felt all right. His dad watched him too, but didn't say much. And Jonathon watched Jenny. She'd even touched him once. In the bus line.

"You still wanna come over Saturday?"

Jonathon almost melted again. "Yeah. For sure."

Then she touched him. Reached out and sort of gently shoved him on the arm. At the top. "See ya then."

"Lookin' good." Jacko smashed into him from the rear. "A shoooore thing."

This time Jonathon managed to twist his arm up his back before he could escape.

Since the last time, Jonathon had thought it best not to practise melting any more. Instead, he decided to wear fewer clothes. That way he could at least get his jeans off. Board shorts actually. Over thongs. Perfect. He wondered why he hadn't thought of it before.

He gazed at his reflection. Button-up shirt (easy to undo), board shorts (Velcro front), baggy undies and thongs. Somehow it didn't look right. It was cold, too. Maybe a jumper over the top would help. Jonathon pulled on his sweatshirt. Nope. Jumpers would have to get dragged off. He needed a cardigan.

"Hey, Dad!"

No answer. Jonathon cruised into the lounge-room.

"Where are you going?" Mr Jones sat up.

"Round to Jenny Sommerville's. I told you."

"She live in the tropics or what?"

"You'll be too cold, Jonathon." Mrs Jones looked worried.

"Nah. I'm OK. Hey, Dad, can I borrow a cardigan?"

Mr Jones looked at him. "Yeah, sure. You want some socks and sandals to go with the rest of the outfit?"

"Oh, come on, Dad. Just a cardigan."

"Where are all your sweatshirts?" Mrs Jones put down her book.

"No, no." Mr Jones stood up. "He's worn them once already. Haven't you, Jonno? Wouldn't do to see him in the same jumper twice."

He disappeared into the bedroom and reappeared with the most horrendous hand-knitted cardigan Jonathon had ever seen. With a V neck. Dad had done well.

"That's nice, Kevin," Jonathon's mum said when she saw it. "How come you never wear it? I made that for you years ago."

"I've been saving it," Mr Jones said, "for a special occasion. Right, Jonno. Here you are, my son. Put it on. Let's see how it looks."

Jonathon put it on.

"Perfect." Mr Jones was really enjoying this. "See, dear, it covers his little bottom and all. Sure you don't want the socks? Sandals? Beanie?"

Jonathon heaved the cardigan up and rolled it around his middle. It slid straight down again. He decided not to check the mirror. He really didn't want to know. He kissed his mum goodbye and opened the door.

"Do you want a brolly?" Mr Jones beamed at him. "No? Well, have a great time."

"See ya, Dad."

One day, Jonathon vowed, he'd get him for this.

By the time he got to Jenny's place the cardigan had stretched down until it was almost level with his boardies. He knocked at the door, rolled up the cardigan, pinned his arms to his sides and hoped for the best. The outside light went on and the door was opened by an attractive middle-aged version of Jenny.

"Hi," she said. "You must be Jonathon. Love your cardigan. Where'd you get it?"

Jonathon followed her inside. "Dad gave it to me."

"David." Mrs Sommerville indicated a man sitting in much the same position as his own father. "David, this is Jenny's friend, Jonathon."

Jonathon reached over to shake hands. Down went the cardigan.

"G'day, Jonathon. That's some cardigan. Your mum knit it for you?"

"No." Jonathon hitched it up again. "She made it for Dad."

"That figures. I've got one just like it. Could you use another one?"

"Don't be ridiculous," interrupted Mrs Sommerville. "Of course Jonathon doesn't want your old cardigan. Do you, Jonathon?"

Before Jonathon could answer, Jenny came in. She took one look at him and shrieked. "Wow! Where'd you get that? Didn't you have one like that, Dad?"

"OK. Enough." Mr Sommerville patted Jonathon on the shoulder. "I think Jon's about had it with the cardigan conversation." Jonathon loved this man. "Sit down and tell me about the canoeing adventures you had."

So Jenny remembered that day, too. She smiled at him. And before he knew it Jonathon was enjoying himself. He especially enjoyed Jenny sitting close to him on the couch. Really close.

The first video was pretty rotten but it didn't matter. Mrs Sommerville kept saying funny things which made it bearable. The second was better. A real night of horrors.

Mrs Sommerville stood up. "I can't stand these movies." She collected her coffee cup. "Goodnight all. Jonathon, great to meet you. Hope we see you again. David, you coming to bed?"

"Yep. One crummy movie a night's enough for me." Mr Sommerville scratched his head. "Jon, see you next time. Just yell if you want a mate for your cardigan."

Jonathon laughed.

"Your mum and dad are really nice," he said as he wriggled back on to the couch. Jenny curled her legs up and he found it very easy to tip her towards him. She snuggled closer. Jonathon snuggled back. He got lost in the scent of her hair.

Suddenly she sat bolt upright. "There," she said, pointing. "How did they do that?"

"What?"

"Hang on." She pressed the rewind button. "Now watch."

Everybody's favourite hero was protecting the love of his life by hiding with her behind a couch. He had on his American high school jacket, jeans, shirt and the usual trimmings. She had on a ski-suit with a hood, for God's sake. Sure enough, next scene: naked. Still behind the couch.

"Now." Jenny flung herself back. "How'd they do that?"

"What?" Jonathon wasn't really listening. He was enjoying the prospect of kissing her. Nothing else seemed very important.

"How do they get all their clothes off lying down like that?"

"Jenny." She turned to face him. "I honestly don't know." He kissed her for a long, long time. Then he stopped to untangle his cardigan from a cushion. "But I'm sure," he said before he kissed her again, "that it's not as hard as it looks."

Also in Plus

OVERLORD
Christopher Hudson and Stuart Cooper

Tom Beddows, a young infantryman, writes in his diary of the true horror of war. The brutal training, the boredom and the sudden fear, the pity and the panic and most of all – the constant presence of death.

A sensitive, yet grim, story of one ordinary fighting man's experience of the greatest conflict in world history. The book of the award-winning film of the same title.

THE ROAD TO MEMPHIS
Mildred D. Taylor

1941 – all America is filled with rumblings of war in Europe and the Pacific. But Cassie Logan has reason to be more concerned with trouble back home in Mississippi. In this new story about the Logan family, Cassie is finishing high school in the city of Jackson and dreaming of college and law school. But no amount of schooling could prepare her for the tense dramas that are about to converge: a quarrel between two young lovers; a black friend's rage at his white tormentors and a white youth's remorse over his part in a violent incident.

Caught up in the centre, Cassie is propelled into three harrowing, exhilarating, unforgettable days that force her to confront the adult world as never before.

MIGHTIER THAN THE LIPSTICK
Ed. Susan Adler

Astute, poignant and sensitive, this is a selection of stories by women from across the globe. There's the agony of dieting, a new look at the relationship between Ms Snow White and the seven dwarfs, the pain of losing a child and the freshness of an eager young woman arriving in a new city.

Including stories by Rosario Ferré, Margaret Sutherland, Ravinder Randhawa, Kate Pullinger and Leonora Brito, this international collection of stories provides a stimulating introduction to the wealth of women's writing today.

DAZ 4 ZOE
Robert Swindells

'Here is a teenage novel with everything: love, loyalty, nail-biting suspense, some excellent writing, and a huge moral poser about where our Two Nations society will end. Set in a not-so-distant future world, the story is told through the alternate voices of the two young lovers. How the two teenagers meet and keep contact across the divide is nail-biting enough, but the story of their escape from the ties of their own communities and the security forces is brilliant, pulling few punches about the cost to others which their freedom must exact' – Aisling Foster, *Independent*

TAKING THE FERRY HOME
Pam Conrad

Ali is instantly wildly jealous of Simone's beauty, wealth and confidence. But Simone is determined that the two should be friends for the summer. And so they become, for a seemingly perfect holiday of fun, friendship and romance. Simone even promises to help Ali get the gorgeous Brendan. But promises are hard for Simone.

In a dramatic climax to this gripping novel, Ali begins to realize that Simone's life isn't to be envied after all.

MADAME DOUBTFIRE
Anne Fine

Lydia, Christopher and Natalie Hilliard are used to domestic turmoil and have been torn between their warring parents ever since the divorce. But all that changes when their mother takes on a most unusual cleaning lady. Despite her extraordinary appearance, Madame Doubtfire turns out to be a talented and efficient housekeeper and, for a short time at least, the arrangement is a resounding success. But as the Hilliard children soon discover, there's more to Madame Doubtfire than domestic talents ...

ROUND BEHIND THE ICE-HOUSE
Anne Fine

Tom wants to forget – to get back into the past when he and Cass were still so close. What are the secrets she is keeping from him? Tom has to face the fact that as he and Cass grow up, they have to grow apart. He may be her twin brother but he doesn't own her and he never can. A powerful and unusual story about the tensions of changing relationships.

MEL
Liz Berry

Seventeen-year-old Melody is desperate for her life to change, but she isn't prepared for the turmoil into which she is thrown following her mother's nervous breakdown. Left alone in their squalid house, Mel determines to repair and redecorate. Then, while searching for furniture in a local junk shop, she meets the dangerously attractive Mitch Hamilton, lead guitarist with top rock group, Assassination. Mitch is keen to help with the house, but Mel is suspicious of his enthusiasm. So when Mitch announces his intention to marry Mel, no one is more astounded than Mel herself. Except Mitch's jealous ex-girlfriend.

A PACK OF LIES
Geraldine McCaughrean

Ailsa doesn't usually pick up men in public libraries – but then MCC Berkshire is rather out of the ordinary and has a certain irresistible charm. Once inside Ailsa and her mother's antiques shop, he also reveals an amazing talent for holding customers spellbound with his extravagant stories – and selling antiques into the bargain!